S0-AAA-361

THE TOR DOUBLES

Tor is proud to bring you the best in science fiction's short novels. An amazing amount of particularly fine science fiction is written at a length just too short to put in a book by itself, so we're providing them two at a time.

The Tor Doubles will be both new stories and older ones, all carefully chosen. Whichever side you start with, you will be able to turn the book over and enjoy the other side just as much.

"Which was your city?" they asked. New York, he told them. "And when was it? The seventh century, did you say?" The twentieth, he told them. They exchanged glances and nodded. "We will have to do it," they said. "The World Trade Center, the Empire State Building, the Citicorp Center, the Cathedral of St. John the Divine: how fascinating! Yankee Stadium. The Verrazano Bridge. We will do it all. But first must come Mohenjo-daro. And then, I think, Constantinople. Did your city have many people?" Seven million, he said. Just in the five boroughs alone. They nodded, smiling amiably, unfazed by the number.

Seven million, seventy million—it was all the same to them, he sensed. They would bring forth the temporaries in whatever quantity was required. He wondered how well they would bring it off.

The Tor Double Novels

*forthcoming

ROBERT SILVERBERG
SAILING TO BYZANTIUM

A TOM DOHERTY ASSOCIATES BOOK
NEW YORK

This is a work of fiction. All the characters and events portrayed in this book are fictitious, and any resemblance to real people or events is purely coincidental.

SAILING TO BYZANTIUM

Copyright © 1985 by Agberg Ltd.

All rights reserved, including the right to reproduce this book or portions thereof in any form.

A TOR Book
Published by Tom Doherty Associates, Inc.
49 West 24 Street
New York, NY 10010

Cover art copyright © 1989 by Brian Waugh. Used by permission of the Luserke Agency.

ISBN: 0-812-50079-2   Can. ISBN: 0-812-55924-X

First Tor edition: July 1989

Printed in the United States of America

0 9 8 7 6 5 4 3 2 1

At dawn he arose and stepped out onto the patio for his first look at Alexandria, the one city he had not yet seen. That year the five cities were Chang-an, Asgard, New Chicago, Timbuctoo, Alexandria: the usual mix of eras, cultures, realities. He and Gioia, making the long flight from Asgard in the distant north the night before, had arrived late, well after sundown, and had gone straight to bed. Now, by the gentle apricot-hued morning light, the fierce spires and battlements of Asgard seemed merely something he had dreamed.

The rumor was that Asgard's moment was finished, anyway. In a little while, he had heard, they were going to tear it down and replace it, elsewhere, with Mohenjo-daro. Though there were never more than five cities, they changed constantly. He could remember a time when they had had Rome of the Caesars instead of Chang-an, and Rio de Janeiro rather than Alexandria. These people saw no point in keeping anything very long.

It was not easy for him to adjust to the sultry intensity of Alexandria after the frozen

splendors of Asgard. The wind, coming off the
water, was brisk and torrid both at once. Soft
turquoise wavelets lapped at the jetties. Strong
presences assailed his senses: the hot heavy
sky, the stinging scent of the red lowland sand
borne on the breeze, the sullen swampy aroma
of the nearby sea. Everything trembled and
glimmered in the early light. Their hotel was
beautifully situated, high on the northern
slope of the huge artificial mound known as
the Paneium that was sacred to the goat-footed
god. From here they had a total view of the
city: the wide noble boulevards, the soaring
obelisks and monuments, the palace of Hadrian just below the hill, the stately and awesome Library, the temple of Poseidon, the
teeming marketplace, the royal lodge that
Mark Antony had built after his defeat at Ac-
tium. And of course the Lighthouse, the wondrous many-windowed Lighthouse, the seventh
wonder of the world, that immense pile of
marble and limestone and reddish-purple As-
wan granite rising in majesty at the end of its
mile-long causeway. Black smoke from the
beacon-fire at its summit curled lazily into the
sky. The city was awakening. Some temporaries in short white kilts appeared and began to
trim the dense dark hedges that bordered the
great public buildings. A few citizens wearing
loose robes of vaguely Grecian style were
strolling in the streets.

There were ghosts and chimeras and phan-
tasies everywhere about. Two slim elegant
centaurs, a male and a female, grazed on the

hillside. A burly thick-thighed swordsman appeared on the porch of the temple of Poseidon holding a Gorgon's severed head; he waved it in a wide arc, grinning broadly. In the street below the hotel gate three small pink sphinxes, no bigger than housecats, stretched and yawned and began to prowl the curbside. A larger one, lion-sized, watched warily from an alleyway: their mother, surely. Even at this distance he could hear her loud purring.

Shading his eyes, he peered far out past the Lighthouse and across the water. He hoped to see the dim shores of Crete or Cyprus to the north, or perhaps the great dark curve of Anatolia. *Carry me toward that great Byzantium,* he thought. *Where all is ancient, singing at the oars.* But he beheld only the endless empty sea, sun-bright and blinding though the morning was just beginning. Nothing was ever where he expected it to be. The continents did not seem to be in their proper places any longer. Gioia, taking him aloft long ago in her little flitterflitter, had shown him that. The tip of South America was canted far out into the Pacific; Africa was weirdly foreshortened; a broad tongue of ocean separated Europe and Asia. Australia did not appear to exist at all. Perhaps they had dug it up and used it for other things. There was no trace of the world he once had known. This was the fiftieth century. "The fiftieth century after *what?*" he had asked several times, but no one seemed to know, or else they did not care to say.

"Is Alexandria very beautiful?" Gioia called from within.

"Come out and see."

Naked and sleepy-looking, she padded out onto the white-tiled patio and nestled up beside him. She fit neatly under his arm. "Oh, yes, yes!" she said softly. "So very beautiful, isn't it? Look, there, the palaces, the Library, the Lighthouse! Where will we go first? The Lighthouse, I think. Yes? And then the marketplace—I want to see the Egyptian magicians—and the stadium, the races—will they be having races today, do you think? Oh, Charles, I want to see everything!"

"Everything? All on the first day?"

"All on the first day, yes," she said. "Everything."

"But we have plenty of time, Gioia."

"Do we?"

He smiled and drew her tight against his side.

"Time enough," he said gently.

He loved her for her impatience, for her bright bubbling eagerness. Gioia was not much like the rest in that regard, though she seemed identical in all other ways. She was short, supple, slender, dark-eyed, olive-skinned, narrow-hipped, with wide shoulders and flat muscles. They were all like that, each one indistinguishable from the rest, like a horde of millions of brothers and sisters—a world of small, lithe, childlike Mediterraneans, built for juggling, for bull-dancing, for sweet white wine at midday and rough red wine at night. They had the same slim bodies, the same broad mouths, the same great glossy eyes. He had never seen anyone who appeared to be younger than twelve or older than twenty. Gioia was somehow a little different, although he did not quite know how; but he knew that it was for that imperceptible but significant difference that he loved her. And probably that was why she loved him also.

He let his gaze drift from west to east, from the Gate of the Moon down broad Canopus Street and out to the harbor, and off to the tomb of Cleopatra at the tip of long slender Cape Lochias. Everything was here and all of it perfect, the obelisks, the statues and marble colonnades, the courtyards and shrines and groves, great Alexander himself in his coffin of crystal and gold: a splendid gleaming pagan city. But there were oddities—an unmistakable mosque near the public gardens, and what seemed to be a Christian church not far from the Library. And those ships in the harbor, with all those red sails and bristling masts— surely they were medieval, and late medieval at that. He had seen such anachronisms in other places before. Doubtless these people found them amusing. Life was a game for them. They played at it unceasingly. Rome, Alexandria, Timbuctoo—why not? Create an Asgard of translucent bridges and shimmering ice-girt palaces, then grow weary of it and take it away? Replace it with Mohenjo-daro? Why not? It seemed to him a great pity to destroy those lofty Nordic feasting-halls for the sake of building a squat, brutal, sun-baked city of brown brick; but these people did not look at things the way he did. Their cities were only temporary. Someone in Asgard had said that Timbuctoo would be the next to go, with Byzantium rising in its place. Well, why not? Why not? They could have anything they liked. This was the fiftieth century, after all. The only rule was that there could be no more than five cities at once. "Limits," Gioia had informed him solemnly when they first began to travel together, "are very important." But she did not know why, or did not care to say.

He stared out once more toward the sea.

He imagined a newborn city congealing suddenly out of mists, far across the water: shining towers, great domed palaces, golden mosaics. That would be no great effort for them. They could just summon it forth whole out of time, the Emperor on his throne and the Emperor's drunken soldiery roistering in the streets, the brazen clangor of the cathedral gong rolling through the Grand Bazaar, dolphins leaping beyond the shoreside pavilions. Why not? They had Timbuctoo. They had Alexandria. Do you crave Constantinople? Then behold Constantinople! Or Avalon, or Lyonesse, or Atlantic. They could have anything they liked. It is pure Schopenhauer here: the world as will and imagination. Yes! These slender dark-eyed people journeying tirelessly from miracle to miracle. Why not Byzantium next? Yes! Why not? *That is no country for old men*, he thought. *The young in one another's arms, the birds in the trees*—yes! Yes! Anything they liked. They even had him. Suddenly he felt frightened. Questions he had not asked for a long time burst through into his consciousness. *Who am I? Why am I here? Who is this woman beside me?*

"You're so quiet all of a sudden, Charles," said Gioia, who could not abide silence for very long. "Will you talk to me? I want you to talk to me. Tell me what you're looking for out there."

He shrugged. "Nothing."

"Nothing?"

"Nothing in particular."

"I could see you seeing something."

"Byzantium," he said. "I was imagining that I could look straight across the water to Byzantium. I was trying to get a glimpse of the walls of Constantinople."

"Oh, but you wouldn't be able to see as far as that from here. Not really."

"I know."

"And anyway Byzantium doesn't exist."

"Not yet. But it will. Its time comes later on."

"Does it?" she said. "Do you know that for a fact?"

"On good authority. I heard it in Asgard," he told her. "But even if I hadn't, Byzantium would be inevitable, don't you think? Its time would have to come. How could we not do Byzantium, Gioia? We certainly will do Byzantium, sooner or later. I know we will. It's only a matter of time. And we have all the time in the world."

A shadow crossed her face. "Do we? Do we?"

He knew very little about himself, but he knew that he was not one of them. That he knew. He knew that his name was Charles Phillips and that before he had come to live among these people he had lived in the year 1984, when there had been such things as computers and television sets and baseball and jet planes, and the world was full of cities, not merely five but thousands of them, New York and London and Johannesburg and Paris and Liverpool and Bangkok and San Francisco and Buenos Aires and a multitude of others, all at the same time. There had been four and a half billion people in the world then; now he doubted that there were as many as four and a half million. Nearly everything had changed beyond comprehension. The moon still seemed the same, and the sun; but at night he searched in vain for familiar constellations. He had no idea how they had brought him from then to now, or why. It did no good to ask. No one had any answers for him; no one so much as appeared to understand what it was that he was trying to learn. After a time he had stopped asking; after a time he had almost entirely ceased wanting to know.

He and Gioia were climbing the Lighthouse. She scampered ahead, in a hurry as always, and he came along behind her in his more stolid fashion. Scores of other tourists, mostly in groups of two or three, were making their way up the wide flagstone ramps, laughing, calling to one another. Some of them, seeing him, stopped a moment, stared, pointed. He was used to that. He was so much taller than any of them; he was plainly not one of them. When they pointed at him he smiled. Sometimes he nodded a little acknowledgment.

He could not find much of interest in the lowest level, a massive square structure two hundred feet high built of huge marble blocks: within its cool musty arcades were hundreds of small dark rooms, the offices of the Lighthouses's keepers and mechanics, the barracks of the garrison, the stables for the three hundred donkeys that carried the fuel to the lantern far above. None of that appeared inviting to him. He forged onward without halting until he emerged on the balcony that led to the next level. Here the Lighthouse grew narrower and became octagonal: its face, granite now and handsomely fluted, rose in a stunning sweep above him.

Gioia was waiting for him there. "This is for you," she said, holding out a nugget of meat on a wooden skewer. "Roast lamb. Absolutely delicious. I had one while I was waiting for you." She gave him a cup of some cool green sherbet also, and darted off to buy a pomegranate. Dozens of temporaries were roaming the balcony, selling refreshments of all kinds.

He nibbled at the meat. It was charred outside, nicely pink and moist within. While he ate, one of the temporaries came up to him

and peered blandly into his face. It was a
stocky swarthy male wearing nothing but a
strip of red and yellow cloth about its waist.
"I sell meat," it said. "Very fine roast lamb,
only five drachmas."

Phillips indicated the piece he was eating. "I
already have some," he said.

"It is excellent meat, very tender. It has been
soaked for three days in the juices of—"

"Please," Phillips said. "I don't want to buy
any meat. Do you mind moving along?"

The temporaries had confused and baffled
him at first, and there was still much about
them that was unclear to him. They were not
machines—they looked like creatures of flesh
and blood—but they did not seem to be human
beings, either, and no one treated them as if
they were. He supposed they were artificial
constructs, products of a technology so con-
summate that it was invisible. Some appeared
to be more intelligent than others, but all of
them behaved as if they had no more auton-
omy than characters in a play, which was es-
sentially what they were. There were untold
numbers of them in each of the five cities,
playing all manner of roles: shepherds and
swineherds, street-sweepers, merchants, boat-
men, vendors of grilled meats and cool drinks,
hagglers in the marketplace, schoolchil-
dren, charioteers, policemen, grooms, gladiators, monks, artisans, whores and cutpurses,
sailors—whatever was needed to sustain the
illusion of a thriving, populous urban center.
The dark-eyed people, Gioia's people, never

performed work. They were not enough of
them to keep a city's functions going, and in
any case they were strictly tourists, wandering with the wind, moving from city to city as
the whim took them, Chang-an to New Chicago, New Chicago to Timbuctoo, Timbuctoo
to Asgard, Asgard to Alexandria, onward, ever
onward.

The temporary would not leave him alone.
Phillips walked away and it followed him, cor-
nering him against the balcony wall. When
Gioia returned a few minutes later, lips prettily stained with pomegranate juice, the temporary was still hovering about him, trying
with lunatic persistence to sell him a skewer
of lamb. It stood much too close to him, almost nose to nose, great sad cowlike eyes
peering intently into his as it extolled with
mournful mooing urgency the quality of its
wares. It seemed to him that he had had trouble like this with temporaries on one or two
earlier occasions. Gioia touched the creature's
elbow lightly and said, in a short sharp tone
Phillips had never heard her use before, "He
isn't interested. Get away from him." It went
at once. To Phillips she said, "You have to be
firm with them."

"I was trying. It wouldn't listen to me."

"You ordered it to go away, and it refused?"

"I asked it to go away. Politely. Too politely,
maybe."

"Even so," she said. "It should have obeyed
a human, regardless."

"Maybe it didn't think I was human," Phillips suggested. "Because of the way I look. My height, the color of my eyes. It might have thought I was some kind of temporary myself."

"No," Gioia said, frowning. "A temporary won't solicit another temporary. But it won't ever disobey a citizen, either. There's a very clear boundary. There isn't ever any confusion. I can't understand why it went on bothering you." He was surprised at how troubled she seemed: far more so, he thought, than the incident warranted. A stupid device, perhaps miscalibrated in some way, overenthusiastically pushing its wares—what of it? What of it? Gioia, after a moment, appeared to come to the same conclusion. Shrugging, she said. "It's defective, I suppose. Probably such things are more common than we suspect, don't you think?" There was something forced about her tone that bothered him. She smiled and handed him her pomegranate. "Here. Have a bite, Charles. It's wonderfully sweet. They used to be extinct, you know. Shall we go on upward?"

The octagonal midsection of the Lighthouse must have been several hundred feet in height, a grim claustrophobic tube almost entirely filled by the two broad spiraling ramps that wound around the huge building's central well. The ascent was slow: a donkey team was a little way ahead of them on the ramp, plodding along laden with bundles of kindling for the lantern. But at last, just as Phillips was growing winded and dizzy, he and Gioia came out onto the second balcony, the one marking the transition between the octagonal section and the Lighthouse's uppermost storey, which was cylindrical and very slender.

She leaned far out over the balustrade. "Oh, Charles, look at the view! Look at it!"

It was amazing. From one side they could see the entire city, and swampy Lake Mareotis and the dusty Egyptian plain beyond it, and from the other they peered far out into the gray and choppy Mediterranean. He gestured toward the innumerable reefs and shallows that infested the waters leading to the harbor entrance. "No wonder they needed a lighthouse here," he said. "Without some kind of gigantic landmark they'd never have found their way in from the open sea."

A blast of sound, a ferocious snort, erupted just above him. He looked up, startled. Immense statues of trumpet-wielding Tritons jutted from the corners of the Lighthouse at this level; that great blurting sound had come from the nearest of them. A signal, he thought. A warning to the ships negotiating that troubled passage. The sound was produced by some kind of steam-powered mechanism, he realized, operated by teams of sweating temporaries clustered about bonfires at the base of each Triton.

Once again he found himself swept by admiration for the clever way these people carried out their reproductions of antiquity. Or *were* they reproductions, he wondered? He still did not understand how they brought their cities into being. For all he knew, this place was the authentic Alexandria itself, pulled forward out of its proper time just as he himself had been. Perhaps this was the true and original Lighthouse, and not a copy. He had no idea which was the case, nor which would be the greater miracle.

"How do we get to the top?" Gioia asked.

"Over there, I think. That doorway."

The spiraling donkey-ramps ended here. The loads of lantern fuel went higher via a dumb-waiter in the central shaft. Visitors continued by way of a cramped staircase, so narrow at its upper end that it was impossible to turn around while climbing. Gioia, tireless, sprinted ahead. He clung to the rail and labored up and up, keeping count of the tiny window-slits to ease the boredom of the ascent. The count was nearing a hundred when finally he stumbled into the vestibule of the beacon chamber. A dozen or so visitors were crowded into it. Gioia was at the far side, by the wall that was open to the sea.

It seemed to him he could feel the building swaying in the winds, up here. How high were they? Five hundred feet, six hundred, seven? The beacon chamber was tall and narrow, divided by a catwalk into upper and lower sections. Down below, relays of temporaries carried wood from the dumb-waiter and tossed it on the blazing fire. He felt its intense heat from where he stood, at the rim of the platform on which the giant mirror of polished metal was hung. Tongues of flame leaped upward and danced before the mirror, which hurled its dazzling beam far out to sea. Smoke rose through a vent. At the very top was a colossal statue of Poseidon, austere, ferocious, looming above the lantern.

Gioia sidled along the catwalk until she was at his side. "The guide was talking before you came," she said, pointing. "Do you see that place over there, under the mirror? Someone standing there and looking into the mirror gets a view of ships at sea that can't be seen from here by the naked eye. The mirror magnifies things."

"Do you believe that?"

She nodded toward the guide. "It said so. And it also told us that if you look in a certain way, you can see right across the water into the city of Constantinople."

She is like a child, he thought. They all are. He said, "You told me yourself this very morning that it isn't possible to see that far. Besides, Constantinople doesn't exist right now."

"It will," she replied. "*You* said that to me, this very morning. And when it does, it'll be reflected in the Lighthouse mirror. That's the truth. I'm absolutely certain of it." She swung about abruptly toward the entrance of the beacon chamber. "Oh, look, Charles! Here come Nissandra and Aramayne! And there's Hawk! There's Stengard!" Gioia laughed and waved and called out names. "Oh, everyone's here! *Everyone!*"

They came jostling into the room, so many

newcomers that some of those who had been there were forced to scramble down the steps on the far side. Gioia moved among them, hugging, kissing. Phillips could scarcely tell one from another—it was hard for him even to tell which were the men and which the women, dressed as they all were in the same sort of loose robes—but he recognized some of the names. These were her special friends, her set, with whom she had journeyed from city to city on an endless round of gaiety in the old days before he had come into her life. He had met a few of them before, in Asgard, in Rio, in Rome. The beacon-chamber guide, a squat wide-shouldered old temporary wearing a laurel wreath on its bald head, reappeared and began its potted speech, but no one listened to it; they were all too busy greeting one another, embracing, giggling. Some of them edged their way over to Phillips and reached up, standing on tiptoes, to touch their fingertips to his cheek in that odd hello of theirs. "Charles," they said gravely, making two syllables out of the name, as these people often did. "So good to see you again. Such a pleasure. You and Gioia—such a handsome couple. So well suited to each other."

Was that so? He supposed it was.

The chamber hummed with chatter. The guide could not be heard at all. Stengard and Nissandra had visited New Chicago for the water-dancing—Aramayne bore tales of a feast in Chang-an that had gone on for *days*—Hawk and Hekna had been to Timbuctoo to see the arrival of the salt caravan, and were going back there soon—a final party soon to celebrate the end of Asgard that absolutely should not be missed—the plans for the new city, Mohenjo-daro—we have reservations for the opening, we wouldn't pass it up for anything—and, yes, they were definitely going to do Constantinople after that, the planners were already deep into their Byzantium research—so good to see you, you look so beautiful all the time—have you been to the Library yet? The zoo? To the temple of Serapis?—

To Phillips they said, "What do you think of our Alexandria, Charles? Of course you must have known it well in your day. Does it look the way you remember it?" They were always asking things like that. They did not seem to comprehend that the Alexandria of the Lighthouse and the Library was long lost and legendary by his time. To them, he suspected, all the places they had brought back into existence were more or less contemporary. Rome of the Caesars, Alexandria of the Ptolemies, Venice of the Doges, Chang-an of the T'angs, Asgard of the Aesir, none any less real than the next nor any less unreal, each one simply a facet of the distant past, the fantastic immemorial past, a plum plucked from that dark backward and abysm of time. They had no contexts for separating one era from another. To them all the past was one borderless timeless realm. Why then should he not have seen the Lighthouse before, he who had leaped into this era from the New York of 1984? He had never been able to explain it to them. Julius Caesar and Hannibal, Helen of Troy and Charlemagne, Rome of the gladiators and New York of the Yankees and Mets, Gilgamesh and Tristan and Othello and Robin Hood and George Washington and Queen Victoria—to them, all equally real and unreal, none of them any more than bright figures moving about on a painted canvas. The past, the past, the elusive and fluid past—to them it was a single place of infinite accessibility and infinite connectivity. Of course they would think he had seen the Lighthouse before. He knew better than to try again to explain things. "No," he said simply. "This is my first time in Alexandria."

They stayed there all winter long, and possibly some of the spring. Alexandria was not a place where one was sharply aware of the change of seasons, nor did the passage of time itself make itself very evident when one was living one's entire life as a tourist.

During the day there was always something new to see. The zoological garden, for instance: a wondrous park, miraculously green and lush in this hot dry climate, where astounding animals roamed in enclosures so generous that they did not seem like enclosures at all. Here were camels, rhinoceroses, gazelles, ostriches, lions, wild asses; and here too, casually adjacent to those familiar African beasts, were hippogriffs, unicorns, basilisks, and fire-snorting dragons with rainbow scales. Had the original zoo of Alexandria had dragons and unicorns? Phillips doubted it. But this one did; evidently it was no harder for the backstage craftsman to manufacture mythic beasts than it was for them to turn out camels and gazelles. To Gioia and her friends all of them were equally mythical, anyway. They were just as awed by the rhinoceros as by the hippogriff. One was no more strange—nor any less—than the other. So far as Phillips had been able to discover, none of the mammals or birds of his era had survived into this one except for a few cats and dogs, though many had been reconstructed.

And then the Library! All those lost treasures, reclaimed from the jaws of time! Stupendous columned marble walls, airy high-vaulted reading-rooms, dark coiling stacks stretching away to infinity. The ivory handles of seven hundred thousand papyrus scrolls bristling on the shelves. Scholars and librarians gliding quietly about, smiling faint scholarly smiles but plainly preoccupied with serious matters of the mind. They were all temporaries, Phillips realized. Mere props, part of the illusion. But were the scrolls illusions too? "Here we have the complete dramas of Sophocles," said the guide with a blithe wave of its hand, indicating shelf upon shelf of texts. Only seven of his hundred twenty-three plays had survived the successive burnings of the library in ancient times by Romans, Christians, Arabs: were the lost ones here, the *Triptolemus*, the *Nausicaa*, the *Jason*, and all the rest? And would he find here too, miraculously restored to being, the other vanished treasures of ancient literature—the memoirs of Odysseus, Cato's history of Rome, Thucydides' life of Pericles, the missing volumes of Livy? But when he asked if he might explore the stacks, the guide smiled apologetically and said that all the librarians were busy just now. Another time, perhaps? Perhaps, said the guide. It made no difference, Phillips decided. Even if these people somehow had brought back those lost masterpieces of antiquity, how would he read them? He knew no Greek.

The life of the city buzzed and throbbed about him. It was a dazzlingly beautiful place: the vast bay thick with sails, the great avenues running rigidly east–west, north–south, the sunlight rebounding almost audibly from the bright walls of the palaces of kings and gods. They have done this very well, Phillips thought: very well indeed. In the marketplace hard-eyed traders squabbled in half a dozen mysterious languages over the price of ebony, Arabian incense, jade, panther-skins. Gioia bought a dram of pale musky Egyptian perfume in a delicate tapering glass flask. Magicians and jugglers and scribes called out stridently to passersby, begging for a few moments of attention and a handful of coins for their labor. Strapping slaves, black and tawny and some that might have been Chinese, were put up for auction, made to flex their muscles, to bare their teeth, to bare their breasts and thighs to prospective buyers. In the gymnasium naked athletes hurled javelins and discuses, and wrestled with terrifying zeal. Gioia's friend Stengard came rushing up with a gift for her, a golden necklace that would not have embarrassed Cleopatra. An hour later she had lost it, or perhaps had given it away while Phillips was looking elsewhere. She bought another, even finer, the next day. Anyone could have all the money he wanted, simply by asking: it was as easy to come by as air, for these people.

Being here was much like going to the movies, Phillips told himself. A different show every day: not much plot, but the special effects were magnificent and the detail-work could hardly have been surpassed. A megamovie, a vast entertainment that went on all the time and was being played out by the whole population of Earth. And it was all so effortless, so spontaneous: just as when he had gone to a movie he had never troubled to think about the myriad technicians behind the scenes, the cameramen and the costume designers and the set-builders and the electricians and the model-makers and the boom operators, so too here he chose not to question the means by which Alexandria had been set before him. It felt real. It *was* real. When he drank the strong red wine it gave him a pleasant buzz. If he leaped from the beacon chamber of the Lighthouse he suspected he would die, though perhaps he would not stay dead for long: doubtless they had some way of restoring him as often as was necessary. Death did not seem to be a factor in these people's lives.

By day they saw sights. By night he and Gioia went to parties, in their hotel, in seaside villas, in the palaces of the high nobility. The usual people were there all the time, Hawk and Hekna, Aramayne, Stengard and Shelimir, Nissandra, Asoka, Afonso, Protay. At the parties there were five or ten temporaries for every citizen, some as mere servants, others as entertainers or even surrogate guests, mingling freely and a little daringly. But everyone knew, all the time, who was a citizen and who just a temporary. Phillips began to think his own status lay somewhere between. Certainly they treated him with a courtesy that no one ever would give a temporary, and yet there was a condescension to their manner that told him not simply that he was not one of them but that he was someone or something of an altogether different order of existence. That he was Gioia's lover gave him some standing in their eyes, but not a great deal: obviously he was always going to be an outsider, a primitive, ancient and quaint. For that matter he noticed that Gioia herself, though unquestionably a member of the set, seemed to be regarded as something of an outsider, like a tradesman's great-granddaughter in a gathering of Plantagenets. She did not always find out about the best parties in time to attend; her friends did not always reciprocate her effusive greetings with the same degree of warmth; sometimes he noticed her straining to hear some bit of gossip that was not quite being shared with her. Was it because she had taken him for her lover? Or was it the other way around: that she had chosen to be his lover precisely because she was *not* a full member of their caste?

Being a primitive gave him, at least, something to talk about at their parties. "Tell us about war," they said. "Tell us about elections. About money. About disease." They wanted to know everything, though they did not seem to pay close attention: their eyes were quick to glaze. Still, they asked. He described traffic jams to them, and politics, and deodorants, and vitamin pills. He told them about cigarettes, newspapers, subways, telephone directories, credit cards, and basketball.

"Which was your city?" they asked. New York, he told them. "And when was it? The seventh century, did you say?" The twentieth, he told them. They exchanged glances and nodded. "We will have to do it," they said. "The World Trade Center, the Empire State Building, the Citicorp Center, the Cathedral of St. John the Divine: how fascinating! Yankee Stadium. The Verrazzano Bridge. We will do it all. But first must come Mohenjo-daro. And then, I think, Constantinople. Did your city have many people?" Seven million, he said. Just in the five boroughs alone. They nodded, smiling amiably, unfazed by the number.

Seven million, seventy million—it was all the

same to then, he sensed. They would just bring
forth the temporaries in whatever quantity
was required. He wondered how well they
would carry the job off. He was no real judge
of Alexandrias and Asgards, after all. Here
they could have unicorns and hippogriffs in the
zoo, and live sphinxes prowling in the gutters,
and it did not trouble him. Their fanciful Alexandria was as good as history's, or better.
But how sad, how disillusioning it would be,
if the New York that they conjured up had
Greenwich Village uptown and Times Square
in the Bronx, and the New Yorkers, gentle and
polite, spoke with the honeyed accents of Sa-
vannah or New Orleans. Well, that was nothing he needed to brood about just now. Very
likely they were only being courteous when
they spoke of doing his New York. They had
all the vastness of the past to choose from:
Nineveh, Memphis of the Pharaohs, the London of Victoria or Shakespeare or Richard the
Third, Florence of the Medici, the Paris of Ab-
elard and Heloise or the Paris of Louis XIV,
Moctezuma's Tenochtitlan and Atahualpa's
Cuzco; Damascus, St. Petersburg, Babylon,
Troy. And then there were all the cities like
New Chicago, out of time that was time yet
unborn to him but ancient history to them. In
such richness, such an infinity of choices, even
mighty New York might have to wait a long
while for its turn. Would he still be among
them by the time they got around to it? By
then, perhaps, they might have become bored
with him and returned him to his own proper

era. Or possibly he would simply have grown old and died. Even here, he supposed, he would eventually die, though no one else ever seemed to. He did not know. He realized that in fact he did not know anything.

The north wind blew all day long. Vast flocks of ibises appeared over the city, fleeing the heat of the interior, and screeched across the sky with their black necks and scrawny legs extended. The sacred birds, descending by the thousands, scuttered about in every crossroad, pouncing on spiders and beetles, on mice, on the debris of the meat-shops and the bakeries. They were beautiful but annoyingly ubiquitous, and they splashed their dung over the marble buildings; each morning squadrons of temporaries carefully washed it off. Gioia said little to him now. She seemed cool, withdrawn, depressed; and there was something almost intangible about her, as though she were gradually becoming transparent. He felt it would be an intrusion upon her privacy to ask her what was wrong. Perhaps it was only restlessness. She became religious, and presented costly offerings at the temples of Serapis, Isis, Poseidon, Pan. She went to the necropolis west of the city to lay wreaths on the tombs in the catacombs. In a single day she climbed the Lighthouse three times without any sign of fatigue. One afternoon he returned from a visit to the Library and found her naked on the patio; she had anointed herself all over with some aromatic green salve.

Abruptly she said, "I think it's time to leave Alexandria, don't you?"

She wanted to go to Mohenjo-daro, but Mohenjo-daro was not yet ready for visitors. Instead they flew eastward to Chang-an, which they had not seen in years. It was Phillips' suggestion: he hoped that the cosmopolitan gaudiness of the old T'ang capital would lift her mood.

They were to be guests of the Emperor this time: an unusual privilege, which ordinarily had to be applied for far in advance, but Phillips had told some of Gioia's highly placed friends that she was unhappy, and they had quickly arranged everything. Three endlessly bowing functionaries in flowing yellow robes and purple sashes met them at the Gate of Brilliant Virtue in the city's south wall and conducted them to their pavilion, close by the imperial palace and the Forbidden Garden. It was a light, airy place, thin walls of plastered brick braced by graceful columns of some dark, aromatic wood. Fountains played on the roof of green and yellow tiles, creating an unending cool rainfall of recirculating water. The balustrades were of carved marble, the door-fittings were of gold.

There was a suite of private rooms for him, and another for her, though they would share the handsome damask-draped bedroom at the heart of the pavilion. As soon as they arrived Gioia announced that she must go to her rooms to bathe and dress. "There will be a formal reception for us at the palace tonight," she said. "They say the imperial receptions are splendid beyond anything you could imagine. I want to be at my best." The Emperor and all his ministers, she told him, would receive them in the Hall of the Supreme Ultimate; there would be a banquet for a thousand people; Persian dancers would perform, and the celebrated jugglers of Chung-nan. Afterward everyone would be conducted into the fantastic landscape of the Forbidden Garden to view the dragon-races and the fireworks.

He went to his own rooms. Two delicate little maid-servants undressed him and bathed him with fragrant sponges. The pavilion came equipped with eleven temporaries who were to be their servants: soft-voiced unobtrusive cat-like Chinese, done with perfect verisimilitude, straight black hair, glowing skin, epicanthic folds. Phillips often wondered what happened to a city's temporaries when the city's time was over. Were the towering Norse heroes of Asgard being recycled at this moment into wiry dark-skinned Dravidians for Mohenjo-daro? When Timbuctoo's day was done, would its brightly robed black warriors be converted into supple Byzantines to stock the arcades of Constantinople? Or did they simply discard the old temporaries like so many excess props, stash them in warehouses somewhere, and turn out the appropriate quantities of the new model? He did not know; and once when he had asked Gioia about it she had grown uncomfortable and vague. She did not like him to probe for information, and he suspected it was because she had very little to give. These people did not seem to question the workings of their own world; his curiosities were very twentieth-century of him, he was frequently told, in that gently patronizing way of theirs. As his two little maids patted him with their sponges he thought of asking them where they had served before Chang-an. Rio? Rome? Haroun al-Raschid's Baghdad? But these fragile girls, he knew, would only giggle and retreat if he tried to question them. Interrogating temporaries was not only improper, but pointless: it was like interrogating one's luggage.

When he was bathed and robed in rich red silks he wandered the pavilion for a little while, admiring the tinkling pendants of green jade dangling on the portico, the lustrous auburn pillars, the rainbow hues of the intricately interwoven girders and brackets that supported the roof. Then, wearying of his solitude, he approached the bamboo curtain at the entrance to Gioia's suite. A porter and one of the maids stood just within. They indicated that he should not enter, but he scowled at them and they melted from him like snowflakes. A trail of incense led him through the pavilion to Gioia's innermost dressing-room. There he halted, just outside the door.

Gioia sat naked with her back to him at an ornate dressing-table of some rare flame-colored wood inlaid with bands of orange and green porcelain. She was studying herself intently in a mirror of polished bronze held by one of her maids: picking through her scalp with her fingernails, as a woman might do who was searching out her gray hairs.

But that seemed strange. Gray hair, on Gioia? On a citizen? A temporary might display some appearance of aging, perhaps, but surely not a citizen. Citizens remained forever young. Gioia looked like a girl. Her face was smooth and unlined, her flesh was firm, her hair was dark: that was true of all of them, every citizen he had ever seen. And yet there was no mistaking what Gioia was doing. She found a hair, frowned, drew it taut, nodded, plucked it. Another. Another. She pressed the tip of her finger to her cheek as if testing it for resilience. She tugged at the skin below her eyes, pulling it downward. Such familiar little gestures of vanity; but so odd here, he thought, in this world of the perpetually young. Gioia, worried about growing old? Had he simply failed to notice the signs of age on her? Or was it that she worked hard behind his back at concealing them? Perhaps that was it. Was he wrong about the citizens, then? Did they age even as the people of less blessed eras had always done, but simply have better ways of hiding it? How old was she, anyway? Thirty? Sixty? Three hundred?

Gioia appeared satisfied now. She waved the mirror away; she rose; she beckoned for her banquet robes. Phillips, still standing unnoticed by the door, studied her with admiration: the small round buttocks, almost but not quite boyish, the elegant line of her spine, the surprising breadth of her shoulders. No, he thought, she is not aging at all. Her body is still like a girl's. She looks as young as on the day they first had met, however long ago that was—he could not say; it was hard to keep track of time here; but he was sure some years had passed since they had come together. Those gray hairs, those wrinkles and sags for which she had searched just now with such desperate intensity, must all be imaginary, mere artifacts of vanity. Even in this remote future epoch, then, vanity was not extinct. He wondered why she was so concerned with the fear of aging. An affectation? Did all these timeless people take some perverse pleasure in fretting over the possibility that they might be growing old? Or was it some private fear of Gioia's, another symptom of the mysterious depression that had come over her in Alexandria?

Not wanting her to think that he had been spying on her, when all he had really intended was to pay her a visit, he slipped silently away to dress for the evening. She came to him an hour later, gorgeously robed, swaddled from chin to ankles in a brocade of brilliant colors shot through with threads of gold, face painted, hair drawn up tightly and fastened with ivory combs: very much the lady of the court. His servants had made him splendid also, a lustrous black surplice embroidered with golden dragons over a sweeping floor-length gown of shining white silk, a necklace and pendant of red coral, a five-cornered gray felt hat that rose in tower upon tower like a ziggurat. Gioia, grinning, touched her fingertips to his cheek. "You look marvelous!" she told him. "Like a grand mandarin!"

"And you like an empress," he said. "Of some distant land: Persia, India. Here to pay a ceremonial visit on the Son of Heaven." An excess of love suffused his spirit, and, catching her lightly by the wrist, he drew her toward him, as close as he could manage it considering how elaborate their costumes were. But as he bent forward and downward, meaning to brush his lips lightly and affectionately against the tip of her nose, he perceived an unexpected strangeness, an anomaly: the coating of white paint that was her makeup seemed oddly to magnify rather than mask the contours of her skin, highlighting and revealing details he had never observed before. He saw a pattern of fine lines radiating from the corners of her eyes, and the unmistakable beginning of a quirk-mark in her cheek just to the left of her mouth, and perhaps the faint indentation of frown-lines in her flawless forehead. A shiver traveled along the nape of his neck. So it was not affectation, then, that had had her studying her mirror so fiercely. Age was in truth beginning to stake its claim on her, despite all that he had come to believe about these people's agelessness. But a moment later he was not sure. Gioia turned and slid gently half a step back from him—she must have found his stare disturbing—and the lines he had thought he had seen were gone. He searched for them and saw only girlish smoothness once again. A trick of the light? A figment of an overwrought imagination? He was baffled.

"Come," she said. "We mustn't keep the Emperor waiting."

Five mustachioed warriors in armor of white quilting and seven musicians playing cymbals and pipes escorted them to the Hall of the Supreme Ultimate. There they found the full court arrayed: princes and ministers, high officials, yellow-robed monks, a swarm of imperial concubines. In a place of honor to the right of the royal thrones, which rose like gilded scaffolds high above all else, was a little group of stern-faced men in foreign costumes, the ambassadors of Rome and Byzantium, of Arabia and Syria, of Korea, Japan, Tibet, Turkestan. Incense smouldered in enameled braziers. A poet sang a delicate twanging melody, accompanying himself on a small harp. Then the Emperor and Empress entered: two tiny aged people, like waxen images, moving with infinite slowness, taking steps no greater than a child's. There was the sound of trumpets as they ascended their thrones. When the little Emperor was seated—he looked like a doll up there, ancient, faded, shrunken, yet still somehow a figure of extraordinary power—he stretched forth both his hands, and enormous gongs began to sound. It was a scene of astonishing splendor, grand and overpowering.

These are all temporaries, Phillips realized suddenly. He saw only a handful of citizens—

eight, ten, possibly as many as a dozen—
scattered here and there about the vast room.
He knew them by their eyes, dark, liquid,
knowing. They were watching not only the imperial spectacle but also Gioia and him; and
Gioia, smiling secretly, nodding almost imper-
ceptibly to them, was acknowledging their
presence and their interest. But those few
were the only ones in here who were autonomous living beings. All the rest—the entire
splendid court, the great mandarins and pala-
dins, the officials, the giggling concubines, the
haughty and resplendent ambassadors, the
aged Emperor and Empress themselves, were
simply part of the scenery. Had the world ever
seen entertainment on so grand a scale before? All this pomp, all this pageantry, conjured up each night for the amusement of a
dozen or so viewers?

At the banquet the little group of citizens sat
together at a table apart, a round onyx slab
draped with translucent green silk. There
turned out to be seventeen of them in all, including Gioia; Gioia appeared to know all of
them, though none, so far as he could tell, was
a member of her set that he had met before.
She did not attempt introductions. Nor was
conversation at all possible during the meal:
there was a constant astounding roaring din
in the room. Three orchestras played at once
and there were troupes of strolling musicians
also, and a steady stream of monks and their
attendants marched back and forth between
the tables loudly chanting sutras and waving

censers to the deafening accompaniment of
drums and gongs. The Emperor did not de-
scend from his throne to join the banquet; he
seemed to be asleep, though now and then he
waved his hand in time to the music. Gigantic
half-naked brown slaves with broad cheekbones and mouths like gaping pockets brought
forth the food, peacock tongues and breast of
phoenix heaped on mounds of glowing saffron-
colored rice, served on frail alabaster plates.
For chopsticks they were given slender rods
of dark jade. The wine, served in glistening
crystal beakers, was thick and sweet, with an
aftertaste of raisins, and no beaker was allowed to remain empty for more than a moment.

Phillips felt himself growing dizzy: when the
Persian dancers emerged he could not tell
whether there were five of them or fifty, and
as they performed their intricate whirling rou-
tines it seemed to him that their slender
muslin-veiled forms were blurring and merg-
ing one into another. He felt frightened by
their proficiency, and wanted to look away, but
he could not. The Chung-nan jugglers that followed them were equally skillful, equally
alarming, filling the air with scythes, flaming
torches, live animals, rare porcelain vases,
pink jade hatchets, silver bells, gilded cups,
wagon-wheels, bronze vessels, and never missing a catch. The citizens applauded politely but
did not seem impressed. After the jugglers, the
dancers returned, performing this time on
stilts; the waiters brought platters of steaming

meat of a pale lavender color, unfamiliar in taste and texture: filet of camel, perhaps, or haunch of hippopotamus, or possibly some choice chop from a young dragon. There was more wine. Feebly Phillips tried to wave it away, but the servitors were implacable. This was a drier sort, greenish-gold, austere, sharp on the tongue. With it came a silver dish, chilled to a polar coldness, that held shaved ice flavored with some potent smoky-flavored brandy. The jugglers were doing a second turn, he noticed. He thought he was going to be ill. He looked helplessly toward Gioia, who seemed sober but fiercely animated, almost manic, her eyes blazing like rubies. She touched his cheek fondly.

A cool draft blew through the hall: they had opened one entire wall, revealing the garden, the night, the stars. Just outside was a colossal wheel of oiled paper stretched on wooden struts. They must have erected it in the past hour: it stood a hundred fifty feet high or even more, and on it hung lanterns by the thousands, glimmering like giant fireflies. The guests began to leave the hall. Phillips let himself be swept along into the garden, where under a yellow moon strange crook-armed trees with dense black needles loomed ominously. Gioia slipped her arm through his. They went down to a lake of bubbling crimson fluid and watched scarlet flamingo-like birds ten feet tall fastidiously spearing angry-eyed turquoise eels. They stood in awe before a fat-bellied Buddha of gleaming blue tilework, seventy feet high. A horse with a golden mane came prancing by, striking showers of brilliant red sparks wherever its hooves touched the ground. In a grove of lemon trees that seemed to have the power to wave their slender limbs about, Phillips came upon the Emperor, standing by himself and rocking gently back and forth. The old man seized Phillips by the hand and pressed something into his palm, closing his fingers tight about it; when he opened his fist a few moments later he found his palm full of gray irregular pearls. Gioia took them from him and cast them into the air, and they burst like exploding firecrackers, giving off splashes of colored light. A little later, Phillips realized that he was no longer wearing his surplice or his white silken undergown. Gioia was naked too, and she drew him gently down into a carpet of moist blue moss, where they made love until dawn, fiercely at first, then slowly, languidly, dreamily. At sunrise he looked at her tenderly and saw that something was wrong.

"Gioia?" he said doubtfully.

She smiled. "Ah, no. Gioia is with Fenimon tonight. I am Belilala."

"With—Fenimon?"

"They are old friends. She had not seen him in years."

"Ah. I see. And you are—?"

"Belilala," she said again, touching her fingertips to his cheek.

It was not unusual, Belilala said. It happened all the time; the only unusual thing was that it had not happened to him before now. Couples formed, traveled together for a while, drifted apart, eventually reunited. It did not mean that Gioia had left him forever. It meant only that just now she chose to be with Feni- mon. Gioia would return. In the meanwhile he would not be alone. "You and I met in New Chicago," Belilala told him. "And then we saw each other again in Timbuctoo. Have you for- gotten? Oh, yes, I see that you have forgot- ten!" She laughed prettily; she did not seem at all offended.

She looked enough like Gioia to be her sis- ter. But, then, all the citizens looked more or less alike to him. And apart from their physi- cal resemblance, so he quickly came to realize, Belilala and Gioia were not really very simi- lar. There was a calmness, a deep reservoir of serenity, in Belilala that Gioia, eager and vol- atile and ever impatient, did not seem to have. Strolling the swarming streets of Chang-an with Belilala, he did not perceive in her any of Gioia's restless feverish need always to know what lay beyond, and beyond, and beyond even that. When they toured the Hsing-ch'ing Pal- ace, Belilala did not after five minutes begin— as Gioia surely would have done—to seek directions to the Fountain of Hsuan-tsung or the Wild Goose Pagoda. Curiosity did not con- sume Belilala as it did Gioia. Plainly she be- lieved that there would always be enough time for her to see everything she cared to see. There were some days when Belilala chose not to go out at all, but was content merely to remain at their pavilion playing a solitary game with flat porcelain counters, or viewing the flowers of the garden.

He found, oddly, that he enjoyed the respite from Gioia's intense world-swallowing appetites; and yet he longed for her to return. Belilala—beautiful, gentle, tranquil, patient— was too perfect for him. She seemed unreal in her gleaming impeccability, much like one of those Sung celadon vases that appear too flawless to have been thrown and glazed by human hands. There was something a little soulless about her: an immaculate finish outside, emptiness within. Belilala might almost have been a temporary, he thought, though he knew she was not. He could explore the pavilions and palaces of Chang-an with her, he could make graceful conversation with her while they dined, he could certainly enjoy coupling with her; but he could not love her or even contemplate the possibility. It was hard to imagine Belilala worriedly studying herself in a mirror for wrinkles and gray hairs. Belilala would never be any older than she was at this moment; nor could Belilala ever have been any younger. Perfection does not move along an axis of time. But the perfection of Belilala's glossy surface made her inner being impenetrable to him. Gioia was more vulnerable, more obviously flawed—her restlessness, her moodiness, her vanity, her fears—and therefore she was more accessible to his own highly imperfect twentieth-century sensibility.

Occasionally he saw Gioia as he roamed the

city, or thought he did. He had a glimpse of her among the miracle-vendors in the Persian Bazaar, and outside the Zoroastrian temple, and again by the goldfish pond in the Serpentine Park. But he was never quite sure that the woman he saw was really Gioia, and he never could get close enough to her to be certain: she had a way of vanishing as he approached, like some mysterious Lorelei luring him onward and onward in a hopeless chase. After a while he came to realize that he was not going to find her until she was ready to be found.

He lost track of time. Weeks, months, years? He had no idea. In this city of exotic luxury, mystery, and magic all was in constant flux and transition and the days had a fitful, unstable quality. Buildings and even whole streets were torn down of an afternoon and re-erected, within days, far away. Grand new pagodas sprouted like toad-stools in the night. Citizens came in from Asgard, Alexandria, Timbuctoo, New Chicago, stayed for a time, disappeared, returned. There was a constant round of court receptions, banquets, theatrical events, each one much like the one before. The festivals in honor of past emperors and empresses might have given some form to the year, but they seemed to occur in a random way, the ceremony marking the death of T'ai Tsung coming around twice the same year, so it seemed to him, once in a season of snow and again in high summer, and the one honoring the ascension of the Empress Wu being held twice in a single season. Perhaps he had misunderstood something. But he knew it was no use asking anyone.

One day Belilala said unexpectedly, "Shall we go to Mohenjo-daro?"

"I didn't know it was ready for visitors," he replied.

"Oh, yes. For quite some time now."

He hesitated. This had caught him unprepared. Cautiously he said, "Gioia and I were going to go there together, you know."

Belilala smiled amiably, as though the topic under discussion were nothing more than a choice of that evening's restaurant.

"Were you?" she asked.

"It was all arranged while we were still in Alexandria. To go with you instead—I don't know what to tell you, Belilala." Phillips sensed that he was growing terribly flustered. "You know that I'd like to go. With you. But on the other hand I can't help feeling that I shouldn't go there until I'm back with Gioia again. If I ever am." How foolish this sounds, he thought. How clumsy, how adolescent. He found that he was having trouble looking straight at her. Uneasily he said, with a kind of desperation in his voice, "I did promise her—there was a commitment, you understand—a firm agreement that we would go to Mohenjo-daro together—"

"Oh, but Gioia's already there!" said Belilala in the most casual way.

He gaped as though she had punched him. *"What?"*

"She was one of the first to go, after it opened. Months and months ago. You didn't know?" she asked, sounding surprised, but not very. "You really didn't know?"

That astonished him. He felt bewildered, betrayed, furious. His cheeks grew hot, his mouth gaped. He shook his head again and again, trying to clear it of confusion. It was a moment before he could speak. "Already there?" he said at last. "Without waiting for me? After we had talked about going there together—after we had agreed—"

Belilala laughed. "But how could she resist seeing the newest city? You know how impatient Gioia is!"

"Yes. Yes."

He was stunned. He could barely think.

"Just like all short-timers," Belilala said. "She rushes here, she rushes there. She must have it all, now, now, right away, at once, instantly. You ought never expect her to wait for you for anything for very long: the fit seizes her, and off she goes. Surely you must know that about her by now."

"A short-timer?" He had not heard that term before.

"Yes. You knew that. You must have known that." Belilala flashed her sweetest smile. She showed no sign of comprehending his distress. With a brisk wave of her hand she said, "Well, then, shall we go, you and I? To Mohenjo-daro?"

"Of course," Phillips said bleakly.

"When would you like to leave?"

"Tonight," he said. He paused a moment. "What's a short-timer, Belilala?"

Color came to her cheeks. "Isn't it obvious?" she asked.

Had there ever been a more hideous place on the face of the earth than the city of Mohenjo-daro? Phillips found it difficult to imagine one. Nor could he understand why, out of all the cities that had ever been, these people had chosen to restore this one to existence. More than ever they seemed alien to him, unfathomable, incomprehensible.

From the terrace atop the many-towered citadel he peered down into grim claustrophobic Mohenjo-daro and shivered. The stark, bleak city looked like nothing so much as some prehistoric prison colony. In the manner of an uneasy tortoise it huddled, squat and compact, against the gray monotonous Indus River plain: miles of dark burnt-brick walls enclosing miles of terrifying orderly streets, laid out in an awesome, monstrous gridiron pattern of maniacal rigidity. The houses themselves were dismal and forbidding too, clusters of brick cells gathered about small airless courtyards. There were no windows, only small doors that opened not onto the main boulevards but onto the tiny mysterious lanes that ran between the buildings. Who had designed this horrifying metropolis? What harsh, sour souls they must have had, these frightening and frightened folk, creating for themselves in the lush fertile plains of India such a Supreme Soviet of a city!

"How lovely it is," Belilala murmured. "How fascinating!"

He stared at her in amazement.

"Fascinating? Yes," he said. "I suppose so. The same way that the smile of a cobra is fascinating."

"What's a cobra?"

"Poisonous predatory serpent," Phillips told her. "Probably extinct. Or formerly extinct, more likely. It wouldn't surprise me if you people had re-created a few and turned them loose in Mohenjo to make things livelier."

"You sound angry, Charles."

"Do I? That's not how I feel."

"How do you feel, then?"

"I don't know," he said after a long moment's pause. He shrugged. "Lost, I suppose. Very far from home."

"Poor Charles."

"Standing here in this ghastly barracks of a city, listening to you tell me how beautiful it is, I've never felt more alone in my life."

"You miss Gioia very much, don't you?"

He gave her another startled look.

"Gioia has nothing to do with it. She's probably been having ecstasies over the loveliness of Mohenjo just like you. Just like all of you. I suppose I'm the only one who can't find the beauty, the charm. I'm the only one who looks out there and sees only horror, and then wonders why nobody else sees it, why in fact people would set up a place like this for *entertainment*, for *pleasure*—"

Her eyes were gleaming. "Oh, you are angry! You really are!"

"Does that fascinate you too?" he snapped. "A demonstration of genuine primitive emotion? A typical quaint twentieth-century outburst?" He paced the rampart in short quick anguished steps. "Ah. Ah. I think I understand it now, Belilala. Of course: I'm part of your circus, the star of the sideshow. I'm the first experiment in setting up the next stage of it, in fact." Her eyes were wide. The sudden harshness and violence in his voice seemed to be alarming and exciting her at the same time. That angered him even more. Fiercely he went on, "Bringing whole cities back out of time was fun for a while, but it lacks a certain authenticity, eh? For some reason you couldn't bring the inhabitants too; you couldn't just grab a few million prehistorics out of Egypt or Greece or India and dump them down in this era, I suppose because you might have too much trouble controlling them, or because you'd have the problem of disposing of them once you were bored with them. So you had to settle for creating temporaries to populate your ancient cities. But now you've got me. I'm something more real than a temporary, and that's a terrific novelty for you, and novelty is the thing you people crave more than anything else: maybe the *only* thing you crave. And here I am, complicated, unpredictable, edgy, capable of anger, fear, sadness, love, and all those other formerly extinct things. Why settle for picturesque architecture when you can observe picturesque emotion, too? What fun I must be for all of you! And if you decide that I was really interesting, maybe you'll ship me back where I came from and check out a few other ancient types—a Roman gladiator, maybe, or a Renaissance pope, or even a Neanderthal or two—"

"Charles," she said tenderly. "Oh, Charles, Charles, Charles, how lonely you must be, how lost, how troubled! Will you ever forgive me? Will you ever forgive us all?"

Once more he was astounded by her. She sounded entirely sincere, altogether sympathetic. Was she? Was she, really? He was not sure he had ever had a sign of genuine caring from any of them before, not even Gioia. Nor could he bring himself to trust Belilala now. He was afraid of her, afraid of all of them, of their brittleness, their slyness, their elegance. He wished he could go to her and have her take him in her arms; but he felt too much the shaggy prehistoric just now to be able to risk asking that comfort of her.

He turned away and began to walk around the rim of the citadel's massive wall.

"Charles?"

"Let me alone for a little while," he said.

He walked on. His forehead throbbed and there was a pounding in his chest. All stress systems going full blast, he thought; secret glands dumping gallons of inflammatory substances into his bloodstream. The heat, the inner confusion, the repellent look of this place—

Try to understand, he thought. Relax. Look about you. Try to enjoy your holiday in Mohenjo-daro.

He leaned warily outward, over the edge of the wall. He had never seen a wall like this; it must be forty feet thick at the base, he guessed, perhaps even more, and every brick perfectly shaped, meticulously set. Beyond the great rampart, marshes ran almost to the edge of the city, although close by the wall the swamps had been dammed and drained for agriculture. He saw lithe brown farmers down there, busy with their wheat and barley and peas. Cattle and buffaloes grazed a little farther out. The air was heavy, dank, humid. All was still. From somewhere close at hand came the sound of a droning, whining stringed instrument and a steady insistent chanting.

Gradually a sort of peace pervaded him. His anger subsided. He felt himself beginning to grow calm again. He looked back at the city, the rigid interlocking streets, the maze of inner lanes, the millions of courses of precise brickwork.

It is a miracle, he told himself, that this city is here in this place and at this time. And it is a miracle that I am here to see it.

Caught for a moment by the magic within the bleakness, he thought he began to understand Belilala's awe and delight, and he wished now that he had not spoken to her so sharply. The city was alive. Whether it was the actual Mohenjo-daro of thousands upon thousands of years ago, ripped from the past by some wondrous hook, or simply a cunning reproduction, did not matter at all. Real or not, this was the true Mohenjo-daro. It had been dead and now, for the moment, it was alive again. These people, these *citizens*, might be trivial, but reconstructing Mohenjo-daro was no trivial achievement. And that the city that had been reconstructed was oppressive and sinister-looking was unimportant. No one was compelled to live in Mohenjo-daro any more. Its time had come and gone, long ago; those little dark-skinned peasants and craftsmen and merchants down there were mere temporaries, mere inanimate things, conjured up like zombies to enhance the illusion. They did not need his pity. Nor did he need to pity himself. He knew that he should be grateful for the chance to behold these things. Some day, when this dream had ended and his hosts had returned him to the world of subways and computers and income tax and television networks, he would think of Mohenjo-daro as he had once beheld it, lofty walls of tightly woven dark brick under a heavy sky, and he would remember only its beauty.

Glancing back, he searched for Belilala and could not for a moment find her. Then he caught sight of her carefully descending a narrow staircase that angled down the inner face of the citadel wall.

"Belilala!" he called.

She paused and looked his way, shading her eyes from the sun with her hand. "Are you all right?"

"Where are you going?"

"To the baths," she said. "Do you want to come?"

He nodded. "Yes. Wait for me, will you? I'll be right there." He began to run toward her along the top of the wall.

The baths were attached to the citadel: a great open tank the size of a large swimming pool, lined with bricks set on edge in gypsum mortar and waterproofed with asphalt, and eight smaller tanks just north of it in a kind of covered arcade. He supposed that in ancient times the whole complex had had some ritual purpose, the large tank used by common folk and the small chambers set aside for the private ablutions of priests or nobles. Now the baths were maintained, it seemed, entirely for the pleasure of visiting citizens. As Phillips came up the passageway that led to the main bath he saw fifteen or twenty of them lolling in the water or padding languidly about, while temporaries of the dark-skinned Mohenjo-daro type served them drinks and pungent little morsels of spiced meat as though this were some sort of luxury resort. Which was, he realized, exactly what it was. The temporaries wore white cotton loincloths; the citizens were naked. In his former life he had encountered that sort of casual public nudity a few times on visits to California and the south of France, and it had made him mildly uneasy. But he was growing accustomed to it here.

The changing-rooms were tiny brick cubicles connected by rows of closely placed steps to the courtyard that surrounded the central tank. They entered one and Belilala swiftly slipped out of the loose cotton robe that she had worn since their arrival that morning. With arms folded she stood leaning against the wall, waiting for him. After a moment he dropped his own robe and followed her outside. He felt a little giddy, sauntering around naked in the open like this.

On the way to the main bathing area they passed the private baths. None of them seemed to be occupied. They were elegantly constructed chambers, with finely jointed brick floors and carefully designed runnels to drain excess water into the passageway that led to the primary drain. Phillips was struck with admiration for the cleverness of the prehistoric engineers. He peered into this chamber and that to see how the conduits and ventilating ducts were arranged, and when he came to the last room in the sequence he was surprised and embarrassed to discover that it was in use. A brawny grinning man, big-muscled, deep-chested, with exuberantly flowing shoulder-length red hair and a flamboyant, sharply tapering beard, was thrashing about merrily with two women in the small tank. Phillips had a quick glimpse of a lively tangle of arms, legs, breasts, buttocks.

"Sorry," he muttered. His cheeks reddened. Quickly he ducked out, blurting apologies as he went. "Didn't realize the room was occupied—no wish to intrude—"

Belilala had proceeded on down the passageway. Phillips hurried after her. From behind him came peals of cheerful raucous booming laughter and high-pitched giggling and the sound of splashing water. Probably they had not even noticed him.

He paused a moment, puzzled, playing back in his mind that one startling glimpse. Something was not right. Those women, he was fairly sure, were citizens: little slender elfin dark-haired girlish creatures, the standard model. But the man? That great curling sweep of red hair? Not a citizen. Citizens did not affect shoulder-length hair. And *red*? Nor had he ever seen a citizen so burly, so powerfully muscular. Or one with a beard. But he could hardly be a temporary, either. Phillips could conceive no reason why there would be so Anglo-Saxon-looking a temporary at Mohenjo-daro; and it was unthinkable for a temporary to be frolicking like that with citizens, anyway.

"Charles?"

He looked up ahead. Belilala stood at the end of the passageway, outlined in a nimbus of brilliant sunlight. "Charles?" she said again. "Did you lose your way?"

"I'm right here behind you," he said. "I'm coming."

"Who did you meet in there?"

"A man with a beard."

"With a what?"

"A beard," he said. "Red hair growing on his face. I wonder who he is."

"Nobody I know," said Belilala. "The only one I know with hair on his face is you. And yours is black, and you shave it off every day." She laughed. "Come along, now! I see some friends by the pool!"

He caught up with her and they went hand in hand out into the courtyard. Immediately a waiter glided up to them, an obsequious little temporary with a tray of drinks. Phillips waved it away and headed for the pool. He felt terribly exposed: he imagined that the citizens disporting themselves here were staring intently at him, studying his hairy primitive body as though he were some mythical creature, a Minotaur, a werewolf, summoned up for their amusement. Belilala drifted off to talk to someone and he slipped into the water, grateful for the concealment it offered. It was deep, warm, comforting. With swift powerful strokes he breast-stroked from one end to the other.

A citizen perched elegantly on the pool's rim smiled at him. "Ah, so you've come at last, Charles!" Charl-less. Two syllables. Someone from Gioia's set: Stengard, Hawk, Aramayne? He could not remember which one. They were all so much alike.

Phillips returned the man's smile in a half-hearted, tentative way. He searched for something to say and finally asked, "Have you been here long?"

"Weeks. Perhaps months. What a splendid achievement this city is, eh, Charles? Such utter unity of mood—such a total statement of a uniquely single-mined esthetic—"

"Yes. Single-minded is the word," Phillips said drily.

"Gioia's word, actually. Gioia's phrase. I was merely quoting."

Gioia. He felt as if he had been stabbed.

"You've spoken to Gioia lately?" he said.

"Actually, no. It was Hekna who saw her. You do remember Hekna, eh?" He nodded toward two naked women standing on the brick platform that bordered the pool, chatting, delicately nibbling morsels of meat. They could have been twins. "There is Hekna, with your Belilala." Hekna, yes. So this must be Hawk, Phillips thought, unless there has been some recent shift of couples. "How sweet she is, your Belilala," Hawk said. "Gioia chose very wisely when she picked her for you."

Another stab: a much deeper one. "Is that how it was?" he said. "Gioia *picked* Belilala for me?"

"Why, of course!" Hawk seemed surprised. It went without saying, evidently. "What did you think? That Gioia would merely go off and leave you to fend for yourself?"

"Hardly. Not Gioia."

"She's very tender, very gentle, isn't she?"

"You mean Belilala? Yes, very," said Phillips carefully. "A dear woman, a wonderful woman. But of course I hope to get together with Gioia again soon." He paused. "They say she's been in Mohenjo-daro almost since it opened."

"She was here, yes."

"*Was?*"

"Oh, you know Gioia," Hawk said lightly. "She's moved along by now, naturally."

Phillips leaned forward. "Naturally," he said. Tension thickened his voice. "Where has she gone this time?"

"Timbuctoo, I think. Or New Chicago. I forget which one it was. She was telling us that she hoped to be in Timbuctoo for the closing-down party. But then Fenimon had some pressing reason for going to New Chicago. I can't remember what they decided to do." Hawk gestured sadly. "Either way, a pity that she left Mohenjo before the new visitor came. She had such a rewarding time with you, after all: I'm sure she'd have found much to learn from him also."

The unfamiliar term twanged an alarm deep in Phillips' consciousness. "*Visitor?*" he said, angling his head sharply toward Hawk. "What visitor do you mean?"

"You haven't met him yet? Oh, of course, you've only just arrived."

Phillips moistened his lips. "I think I may have seen him. Long red hair? Beard like this?"

"That's the one! Willoughby, he's called. He's—what?—a Viking, a pirate, something like that. Tremendous vigor and force. Remarkable person. We should have many more visitors, I think. They're far superior to temporaries, everyone agrees. Talking with a temporary is a little like talking to one's self, wouldn't you say? They give you no significant illumination. But a visitor—someone like this Willoughby—or like you, Charles—a visitor can be truly enlightening, a visitor can transform one's view of reality—"

"Excuse me," Phillips said. A throbbing began behind his forehead. "Perhaps we can continue this conversation later, yes?" He put the flats of his hands against the hot brick of the platform and hoisted himself swiftly from the pool. "At dinner, maybe—or afterward—yes? All right?" He set off at a quick half-trot back toward the passageway that led to the private baths.

As he entered the roofed part of the structure his throat grew dry, his breath suddenly came short. He padded quickly up the hall and peered into the little bath-chamber. The bearded man was still there, sitting up in the tank, breast-high above the water, with one arm around each of the women. His eyes gleamed with fiery intensity in the dimness. He was grinning in marvelous self-satisfaction; he seemed to brim with intensity, confidence, gusto.

Let him be what I think he is, Phillips prayed. I have been alone among these people long enough.

"May I come in?" he asked.

"Aye, fellow!" cried the man in the tub thunderously. "By my troth, come ye in, and bring your lass as well! God's teeth, I wot there's room aplenty for more folk in this tub than we!''

At that great uproarious outcry Phillips felt a powerful surge of joy. What a joyous rowdy voice! How rich, how lusty, how totally uncitizenlike!

And those oddly archaic words! *God's teeth? By my troth?* What sort of talk was that? What else but the good pure sonorous Elizabethan diction! Certainly it had something of the roll and fervor of Shakespeare about it. And spoken with—an Irish brogue, was it? No, not quite: it was English, but English spoken in no manner Phillips had ever heard.

Citizens did not speak that way. But a *visitor* might.

So it was true. Relief flooded Phillips' soul. Not alone, then! Another relict of a former age—another wanderer—a companion in chaos, a brother in adversity—a fellow voyager, tossed even farther than he had been by the tempests of time—

The bearded man grinned heartily and beckoned to Phillips with a toss of his head. "Well, join us, join us, man! 'Tis good to see an English face again, amidst all these Moors and rogue Portugals! But what have ye done with thy lass? One can never have enough wenches, d'ye not agree?"

The force and vigor of him were extraordinary: almost too much so. He roared, he bellowed, he boomed. He was so very much what he ought to be that he seemed more a character out of some old pirate movie than anything

else, so blustering, so real, that he seemed unreal. A stage-Elizabethan, larger than life, a
boisterous young Falstaff without the belly.

Hoarsely, Phillips said, "Who are you?"

"Why, Ned Willoughby's son Francis am I,
of Plymouth. Late of the service of Her Most
Protestant Majesty, but most foully abducted
by the powers of darkness and cast away
among these blackamoor Hindus, or whatever
they be. And thyself?"

"Charles Phillips." After a moment's uncer-
tainty he added, "I'm from New York."

"*New* York? What place is that? In faith,
man, I know it not!"

"A city in America."

"A city in America, forsooth! What a fine
fancy that is! In America, you say, and not on
the Moon, or perchance underneath the sea?"
To the women Willoughby said, "D'ye hear
him? He comes from a city in America! With
the face of an Englishman, though not the
manner of one, and not quite the proper sort
of speech. A city in America! A *city*. God's
blood, what will I hear next?"

Phillips trembled. Awe was beginning to take
hold of him. This man had walked the streets
of Shakespeare's London, perhaps. He had
clinked canisters with Marlowe or Essex or
Walter Raleigh; he had watched the ships of
the Armada wallowing in the Channel. It
strained Phillips' spirit to think of it. This
strange dream in which he found himself was
compounding its strangeness now. He felt like
a weary swimmer assailed by heavy surf,

winded, dazed. The hot close atmosphere of the baths was driving him toward vertigo. There could be no doubt of it any longer. He was not the only primitive—the only *visitor*— who was wandering loose in this fiftieth century. They were conducting other experiments as well. He gripped the sides of the door to steady himself and said, "When you speak of Her Most Protestant Majesty, it's Elizabeth the First you mean, is that not so?"

"Elizabeth, aye! As to the First, that is true enough, but why trouble to name her thus? There is but one. First and Last, I do trow, and God save her, there is no other!"

Phillips studied the other man warily. He knew that he must proceed with care. A misstep at this point and he would forfeit any chance that Willoughby would take him seriously. How much metaphysical bewilderment, after all, could this man absorb? What did he know, what had anyone of his time known, of past and present and future and the notion that one might somehow move from one to the other as readily as one would go from Surrey to Kent? That was a twentieth-century idea, late nineteenth at best, a fantastical speculation that very likely no one had ever considered before Wells had sent his time traveler off to stare at the reddened sun of the earth's last twilight. Willoughby's world was a world of Protestants and Catholics, of kings and queens, of tiny sailing vessels, of swords at the hip and ox-carts on the road: that world seemed to Phillips far more alien and distant than was this world of citizens and temporaries. The risk that Willoughby would not begin to understand him was great.

But this man and he were natural allies against a world they had never made. Phillips chose to take the risk.

"Elizabeth the First is the queen you serve," he said. "There will be another of her name in England, in due time. Has already been, in fact."

Willoughby shook his head like a puzzled lion. "Another Elizabeth, d'ye say?"

"A second one, and not much like the first. Long after your Virgin Queen, this one. She will reign in what you think of as the days to come. That I know without doubt."

The Englishman peered at him and frowned. "You see the future? Are you a soothsayer, then? A necromancer, mayhap? Or one of the very demons that brought me to this place?"

"Not at all," Phillips said gently. "Only a lost soul, like yourself." He stepped into the little room and crouched by the side of the tank. The two citizen-women were staring at him in bland fascination. He ignored them. To Willoughby he said, "Do you have any idea where you are?"

The Englishman had guessed, rightly enough, that he was in India: "I do believe these little brown Moorish folk are the Hindu sort," he said. But that was as far as his comprehension of what had befallen him could go.

It had not occurred to him that he was no

longer living in the sixteenth century. And of course he did not begin to suspect that this strange and somber brick city in which he found himself was a wanderer out of an era even more remote than his own. Was there any way, Phillips wondered, of explaining that to him?

He had been here only three days. He thought it was devils that had carried him off. "While I slept did they come for me," he said. "Mephistophilis Sathanas and his henchmen seized me—God alone can say why—and swept me in a moment out to this torrid realm from England, where I reposed among friends and family. For I was between one voyage and the next, you must understand, awaiting Drake and his ship—you know Drake, the glorious Francis? God's blood, there's a mariner for ye! We were to go to the Main again, he and I, but instead here I be in this other place—" Willoughby leaned close and said, "I ask you, soothsayer, how can it be, that a man go to sleep in Plymouth and wake up in India? It is passing strange, is it not?"

"That it is," Phillips said.

"But he that is in the dance must needs dance on, though he do but hop, eh? So do I believe." He gestured toward the two citizen-women. "And therefore to console myself in this pagan land I have found me some sport among these little Portugal women—"

"Portugal?" said Phillips.

"Why, what else can they be, but Portugals? Is it not the Portugals who control all these coasts of India? See, the people are of two sorts here, the blackamoors and the others, the fair-skinned ones, the lords and masters who lie here in these baths. If they be not Hindus, and I think they are not, then Portugals is what they must be." He laughed and pulled the women against himself and rubbed his hands over their breasts as though they were fruits on a vine. "Is that not what you are, you little naked shameless Papist wenches? A pair of Portugals, eh?"

They giggled, but did not answer.

"No," Phillips said. "This is India, but not the India you think and know. And these women are not Portuguese."

"Not Portuguese?" Willoughby said, baffled.

"No more so than you. I'm quite certain of that."

Willoughby stroked his beard. "I do admit I found them very odd, for Portugals. I have heard not a syllable of their Portugee speech on their lips. And it is strange also that they run naked as Adam and Eve in these baths, and allow me free plunder of their women, which is not the way of Portugals at home, God wot. But I thought me, this is India, they choose to live in another fashion here—"

"No," Phillips said. "I tell you, these are not Portuguese, nor any other people of Europe who are known to you."

"Prithee, who are they, then?"

Do it delicately, now, Phillips warned himself. *Delicately.*

He said, "It is not far wrong to think of them

as spirits of some kind—demons, even. Or sorcerers who have magicked us out of our proper places in the world." He paused, groping for some means to share with Willoughby, in a way that Willoughby might grasp, this mystery that had enfolded them. He drew a deep breath. "They've taken us not only across the sea," he said, "but across the years as well. We have both been hauled, you and I, far into the days that are to come."

Willoughby gave him a look of blank bewilderment.

"Days that are to come? Times yet unborn, d'ye mean? Why, I comprehend none of that!"

"Try to understand. We're both castaways in the same boat, man! But there's no way we can help each other if I can't make you see—"

Shaking his head, Willoughby muttered, "In faith, good friend, I find your words the merest folly. Today is today, and tomorrow is tomorrow, and how can a man step from one to t'other until tomorrow be turned into today?"

"I have no idea," said Phillips. Struggle was apparent on Willoughby's face; but plainly he could perceive no more than the haziest outline of what Phillips was driving at, if that much. "But this I know," he went on, "that your world and all that was in it is dead and gone. And so is mine, though I was born four hundred years after you, in the time of the second Elizabeth."

Willoughby snorted scornfully. "Four hundred—"

"You must believe me!"

"Nay! Nay!"

"It's the truth. Your time is only history to me. And mine and yours are history to *them*—ancient history. They call us visitors, but what we are is captives." Phillips felt himself quivering in the intensity of his effort. He was aware how insane this must sound to Willoughby. It was beginning to sound insane to him. "They've stolen us out of our proper times—seizing us like gypsies in the night—"

"Fie, man! You rave with lunacy!"

Phillips shook his head. He reached out and seized Willoughby tightly by the wrist. "I beg you, listen to me!" The citizen-women were watching closely, whispering to one another behind their hands, laughing. "Ask them!" Phillips cried. "Make them tell you what century this is! The sixteenth, do you think? Ask them!"

"What century could it be, but the sixteenth of our Lord?"

"They will tell you it is the fiftieth."

Willoughby looked at him pityingly. "Man, man, what a sorry thing thou art! The fiftieth, indeed!" He laughed. "Fellow, listen to me, now. There is but one Elizabeth, safe upon her throne in Westminster. This is India. The year is Anno 1591. Come, let us you and I steal a ship from these Portugals, and make our way back to England, and peradventure you may get from there to your America—"

"There is no England."

"Ah, can you say that and not be mad?"

"The cities and nations we knew are gone.

These people live like magicians, Francis."
There was no use holding anything back now,
Phillips thought leadenly. He knew that he had
lost. "They conjure up places of long ago, and
build them here and there to suit their fancy,
and when they are bored with them they destroy them, and start anew. There is no England. Europe is empty, featureless, void. Do
you know what cities there are? There are only
five in all the world. There is Alexandria of
Egypt. There is Timbuctoo in Africa. There is
New Chicago in America. There is a great city
in China—in Cathay, I suppose you would
say. And there is this place, which they call
Mohenjo-daro, and which is far more ancient
than Greece, than Rome, than Babylon."

Quietly Willoughby said, "Nay. This is mere
absurdity. You say we are in some far tomorrow, and then you tell me we are dwelling in
some city of long ago."

"A conjuration, only," Phillips said in desperation. "A likeness of that city. Which these
folk have fashioned somehow for their own
amusement. Just as we are here, you and I: to
amuse them. Only to amuse them."

"You are completely mad."

"Come with me, then. Talk with the citizens
by the great pool. Ask them what year this is;
ask them about England; ask them how you
come to be here." Once again Phillips grasped
Willoughby's wrist. "We should be allies. If we
work together, perhaps we can discover some
way to get ourselves out of this place, and—"

"Let me be, fellow."

"Please—"

"Let me be!" roared Willoughby, and pulled his arm free. His eyes were stark with rage. Rising in the tank, he looked about furiously as though searching for a weapon. The citizen-women shrank back away from him, though at the same time they seemed captivated by the big man's fierce outburst. "Go to, get you to Bedlam! Let me be, madman! Let me be!"

Dismally Phillips roamed the dusty unpaved streets of Mohenjo-daro alone for hours. His failure with Willoughby had left him bleak-spirited and somber: he had hoped to stand back to back with the Elizabethan against the citizens, but he saw now that that was not to be. He had bungled things; or, more likely, it had been impossible ever to bring Willoughby to see the truth of their predicament.

In the stifling heat he went at random through the confusing congested lanes of flat-roofed, windowless houses and blank, feature-less walls until he emerged into a broad marketplace. The life of the city swirled madly around him: the pseudo-life, rather, the intricate interactions of the thousands of temporaries who were nothing more than wind-up dolls set in motion to provide the illusion that pre-Vedic India was still a going concern. Here vendors sold beautiful little carved stone seals portraying tigers and monkeys and strange humped cattle, and women bargained vociferously with craftsmen for ornaments of ivory, gold, copper, and bronze. Weary-looking women squatted behind immense mounds of newly made pottery, pinkish-red with black designs. No one paid any attention to him. He was the outsider here, neither citizen nor temporary. They belonged.

He went on, passing the huge granaries where workmen ceaselessly unloaded carts of wheat and others pounded grain on great circular brick platforms. He drifted into a public restaurant thronging with joyless silent people standing elbow to elbow at small brick counters, and was given a flat round piece of bread, a sort of tortilla or chapatti, in which was stuffed some spiced mincemeat that stung his lips like fire. Then he moved onward, down a wide, shallow, timbered staircase into the lower part of the city, where the peasantry lived in cell-like rooms packed together as though in hives.

It was an oppressive city, but not a squalid one. The intensity of the concern with sanitation amazed him: wells and fountains and public privies everywhere, and brick drains running from each building, leading to covered cesspools. There was none of the open sewage and pestilent gutters that he knew still could be found in the India of his own time. He wondered whether ancient Mohenjo-daro had in truth been so fastidious. Perhaps the citizens had redesigned the city to suit their own ideals of cleanliness. No: most likely what he saw was authentic, he decided, a function of the same obsessive discipline that had given the city its rigidity of form. If Mohenjo-daro had been a verminous filthy hole, the citizens probably would have re-created it in just that way, and loved it for its fascinating, reeking filth.

Not that he had ever noticed an excessive concern with authenticity on the part of the citizens; and Mohenjo-daro, like all the other restored cities he had visited, was full of the usual casual anachronisms. Phillips saw images of Shiva and Krishna here and there on the walls of buildings he took to be temples, and the benign face of the mother-goddess Kali loomed in the plazas. Surely those deities had arisen in India long after the collapse of the Mohenjo-daro civilization. Were the citizens indifferent to such matters of chronology? Or did they take a certain naughty pleasure in mixing the eras—a mosque and a church in Greek Alexandria, Hindu gods in prehistoric Mohenjo-daro? Perhaps their records of the past had become contaminated with errors over the thousands of years. He would not have been surprised to see banners bearing portraits of Gandhi and Nehru being carried in procession through the streets. And there were phantasms and chimeras at large here again too, as if the citizens were untroubled by the boundary between history and myth: little fat elephant-headed Ganeshas blithely plunging their trunks into water-fountains, a six-armed three-headed woman sunning herself on a brick terrace. Why not? Surely that was the motto of these people: *Why not, why not, why not?* They could do as they pleased, and they did. Yet Gioia had said to him, long ago, "Limits are very important." In what, Phillips wondered, did they limit themselves, other than the number of their cities? Was there a quota, perhaps, on the number of "visitors" they allowed themselves to kidnap from the past? Until today he had thought he was the only one; now he knew there was at least one other; possibly there were more elsewhere, a step or two ahead or behind him, making the circuit with the citizens who traveled endlessly from New Chicago to Chang-an to Alexandria. We should join forces, he thought, and compel them to send us back to our rightful eras. *Compel?* How? File a class-action suit, maybe? Demonstrate in the streets? Sadly he thought of his failure to make common cause with Willoughby. We are natural allies, he thought. Together perhaps we might have won some compassion from these people. But to Willoughby it must be literally unthinkable that Good Queen Bess and her subjects were sealed away on the far side of a barrier hundreds of centuries thick. He would prefer to believe that England was just a few months' voyage away around the Cape of Good Hope, and that all he need do was commandeer a ship and set sail for home. Poor Willoughby: probably he would never see his home again.

The thought came to Phillips suddenly:

Neither will you.

And then, after it:

If you could go home, would you really want to?

One of the first things he had realized here was that he knew almost nothing substantial about his former existence. His mind was well stocked with details on life in twentieth-century New York, to be sure; but of himself he could say not much more than that he was Charles Phillips and had come from 1984. Profession? Age? Parents' names? Did he have a wife? Children? A cat, a dog, hobbies? No data: none. Possibly the citizens had stripped such things from him when they brought him here, to spare him from the pain of separation. They might be capable of that kindness. Knowing so little of what he had lost, could he truly say that he yearned for it? Willoughby seemed to remember much more of his former life, and longed for it and more. He was spared that. Why not stay here, and go on and on from city to city, sightseeing all of time past as the citizens conjured it back into being? Why not? Why not? The chances were that he had no choice about it, anyway.

He made his way back up toward the citadel and to the baths once more. He felt a little like a ghost, haunting a city of ghosts.

Belilala seemed unaware that he had been gone for most of the day. She sat by herself on the terrace of the baths, placidly sipping some thick milky beverage that had been sprinkled with a dark spice. He shook his head when she offered him some.

"Do you remember I mentioned that I saw a man with red hair and a beard this morning?"

Phillips said. "He's a visitor. Hawk told me that."

"Is he?" Belilala asked.

"From a time about four hundred years before mine. I talked with him. He thinks he was brought here by demons." Phillips gave her a searching look. "I'm a visitor too, isn't that so?"

"Of course, love."

"And how was *I* brought here? By demons also?"

Belilala smiled indifferently. "You'd have to ask someone else. Hawk, perhaps. I haven't looked into these things very deeply."

"I see. Are there many visitors here, do you know?"

A languid shrug. "Not many, no, not really. I've only heard of three or four besides you. There may be others by now, I suppose." She rested her hand lightly on his. "Are you having a good time in Mohenjo, Charles?"

He let her question pass as though he had not heard it.

"I asked Hawk about Gioia," he said.

"Oh?"

"He told me that she's no longer here, that she's gone on to Timbuctoo or New Chicago, he wasn't sure which."

"That's quite likely. As everybody knows, Gioia rarely stays in the same place very long."

Phillips nodded. "You said the other day that Gioia is a short-timer. That means she's going to grow old and die, doesn't it?"

"I thought you understood that, Charles."

"Whereas you will not age? Nor Hawk, nor Stengard, nor any of the rest of your set?"

"We will live as long as we wish," she said. "But we will not age, no."

"What makes a person a short-timer?"

"They're born that way, I think. Some missing gene, some extra gene—I don't actually know. It's extremely uncommon. Nothing can be done to help them. It's very slow, the aging. But it can't be halted."

Phillips nodded. "That must be very disagreeable," he said. "To find yourself one of the few people growing old in a world where everyone stays young. No wonder Gioia is so impatient. No wonder she runs around from place to place. No wonder she attaches herself so quickly to the barbaric hairy visitor from the twentieth century, who comes from a time when *everybody* was a short-timer. She and I have something in common, wouldn't you say?"

"In a manner of speaking, yes."

"We understand aging. We understand death. Tell me: is Gioia likely to die very soon, Belilala?"

"Soon? Soon?" She gave him a wide-eyed child-like stare. "What is soon? How can I say? What you think of as soon and what I think of as soon are not the same things, Charles." Then her manner changed: she seemed to be hearing what he was saying for the first time. Softly she said, "No, no, Charles. I don't think she will die very soon."

"When she left me in Chang-an, was it because she had become bored with me?"

Belilala shook her head. "She was simply restless. It had nothing to do with you. She was never bored with you."

"Then I'm going to go looking for her. Wherever she may be, Timbuctoo, New Chicago, I'll find her. Gioia and I belong together."

"Perhaps you do," said Belilala. "Yes. Yes, I think you really do." She sounded altogether unperturbed, unrejected, unbereft. "By all means, Charles. Go to her. Follow her. Find her. Wherever she may be."

They had already begun dismantling Timbuctoo when Phillips got there. While he was still high overhead, his flitterflitter hovering above the dusty tawny plain where the River Niger met the sands of the Sahara, a surge of keen excitement rose in him as he looked down at the square gray flat-roofed mud-brick buildings of the great desert capital. But when he landed he found gleaming metal-skinned robots swarming everywhere, a horde of them scuttling about like giant shining insects, pulling the place apart.

He had not known about the robots before. So that was how all these miracles were carried out, Phillips realized: an army of obliging machines. He imagined them bustling up out of the earth whenever their services were needed, emerging from some sterile subterranean storehouse to put together Venice or Thebes or Knossos or Houston or whatever place was required, down to the finest detail, and then at some later time returning to undo everything that they had fashioned. He watched them now, diligently pulling down the adobe walls, demolishing the heavy metal-studded gates, bulldozing the amazing labyrinth of alleyways and thoroughfares, sweeping away the market. On his last visit to Timbuctoo that market had been crowded with a horde of veiled Tuaregs and swaggering Moors, black Sudanese, shrewd-faced Syrian traders, all of them busily dickering for camels, horses, donkeys, slabs of salt, huge green melons, silver bracelets, splendid vellum Korans. They were all gone now, that picturesque crowd of swarthy temporaries. Nor were there any citizens to be seen. The dust of destruction choked the air. One of the robots came up to Phillips and said in a dry crackling insect-voice, "You ought not to be here. This city is closed."

He stared at the flashing, buzzing band of scanners and sensors across the creature's glittering tapered snout. "I'm trying to find someone, a citizen who may have been here recently. Her name is—"

"This city is closed," the robot repeated inexorably.

They would not let him stay as much as an hour. There is no food here, the robot said, no water, no shelter. This is not a place any longer. You may not stay. You may not stay. You may not stay.

This is not a place any longer.

Perhaps he could find her in New Chicago, then. He took to the air again, soaring northward and westward over the vast emptiness. The land below him curved away into the hazy horizon, bare, sterile. What had they done with the vestiges of the world that had gone before? Had they turned their gleaming metal beetles loose to clean everything away? Were there no ruins of genuine antiquity anywhere? No scrap of Rome, no shard of Jerusalem, no stump of Fifth Avenue? It was all so barren down there: an empty stage, waiting for its next set to be built. He flew in a great arc across the jutting hump of Africa and on into what he supposed was southern Europe: the little vehicle did all the work, leaving him to doze or stare as he wished. Now and again he saw another flitter-flitter pass by, far away, a dark distant winged teardrop outlined against the hard clarity of the sky. He wished there was some way of making radio contact with them, but he had no idea how to go about it. Not that he had anything he wanted to say; he wanted only to hear a human voice. He was utterly isolated. He might just as well have been the last living man on Earth. He closed his eyes and thought of Gioia.

"Like this?" Phillips asked. In an ivory-paneled oval room sixty stories above the softly glowing streets of New Chicago he touched a small cool plastic canister to his upper lip and pressed the stud at its base. He heard a foaming sound; and then blue vapor rose to his nostrils.

"Yes," Cantilena said. "That's right."

He detected a faint aroma of cinnamon, cloves, and something that might almost have been broiled lobster. Then a spasm of dizziness hit him and visions rushed through his head: Gothic cathedrals, the Pyramids, Central Park under fresh snow, the harsh brick warrens of Mohenjo-daro, and fifty thousand other places all at once, a wild roller-coaster ride through space and time. It seemed to go on for centuries. But finally his head cleared and he looked about, blinking, realizing that the whole thing had taken only a moment. Cantilena still stood at his elbow. The other citizens in the room—fifteen, twenty of them—had scarcely moved. The strange little man with the celadon skin over by the far wall continued to stare at him.

"Well?" Cantilena asked. "What did you think?"

"Incredible."

"And very authentic. It's an actual New Chicagoan drug. The exact formula. Would you like another?"

"Not just yet," Phillips said uneasily. He swayed and had to struggle for his balance. Sniffing that stuff might not have been such a wise idea, he thought.

He had been in New Chicago a week, or perhaps it was two, and he was still suffering from the peculiar disorientation that the city always aroused in him. This was the fourth time

that he had come here, and it had been the
same every time. New Chicago was the only
one of the reconstructed cities of this world
that in its original incarnation had existed *after* his own era. To him it was an outpost of
the incomprehensible future; to the citizens it
was a quaint simulacrum of the archaeologi-
cal past. That paradox left him aswirl with impossible confusions and tensions.

What had happened to *old* Chicago was of
course impossible for him to discover. Vanished without a trace, that was clear: no Water
Tower, no Marina City, no Hancock Center, no
Tribune building, not a fragment, not an atom.
But it was hopeless to ask any of the million-
plus inhabitants of New Chicago about their
city's predecessor. They were only temporaries; they knew no more than they had to know,
and all that they had to know was how to go
through the motions of whatever it was that
they did by way of creating the illusion that
this was a real city. They had no need of knowing ancient history.

Nor was he likely to find out anything from
a citizen, of course. Citizens did not seem to
bother much about scholarly matters. Phillips
had no reason to think that the world was anything other than an amusement park to them.
Somewhere, certainly, there had to be those
who specialized in serious study of the lost
civilizations of the past—for how, otherwise,
would these uncanny reconstructed cities be
brought into being? "The planners," he had
once heard Nissandra or Aramayne say, "are

already deep into their Byzantium research."
But who were the planners? He had no idea.
For all he knew, they were the robots. Perhaps
the robots were the real masters of this whole
era, who created the cities not primarily for
the sake of amusing the citizens but in their
own diligent attempt to comprehend the life
of the world that had passed away. A wild
speculation, yes; but not without some plau-
sibility, he thought.

He felt oppressed by the party gaiety all
about him. "I need some air," he said to Cantilena, and headed toward the window. It was
the merest crescent, but a breeze came
through. He looked out at the strange city below.

New Chicago had nothing in common with
the old one but its name. They had built it, at
least, along the western shore of a large inland
lake that might even be Lake Michigan, although when he had flown over it it had seemed
broader and less elongated than the lake he
remembered. The city itself was a lacy fantasy
of slender pastel-hued buildings rising at odd
angles and linked by a webwork of gently un-
dulating aerial bridges. The streets were long
parentheses that touched the lake at their
northern and southern ends and arched grace-
fully westward in the middle. Between each of
the great boulevards ran a track for public
transportation—sleek aquamarine bubble-
vehicles gliding on soundless wheels—and
flanking each of the tracks were lush strips of
park. It was beautiful, astonishingly so, but in-

substantial. The whole thing seemed to have been contrived from sunbeams and silk.

A soft voice beside him said, "Are you becoming ill?"

Phillips glanced around. The celadon man stood beside him: a compact, precise person, vaguely Oriental in appearance. His skin was of a curious gray-green hue like no skin Phillips had ever seen, and it was extraordinarily smooth in texture, as though he were made of fine porcelain.

He shook his head. "Just a little queasy," he said. "This city always scrambles me."

"I suppose it can be disconcerting," the little man replied. His tone was furry and veiled, the inflection strange. There was something feline about him. He seemed sinewy, unyielding, almost menacing. "Visitor, are you?"

Phillips studied him a moment. "Yes," he said.

"So am I, of course."

"Are you?"

"Indeed." The little man smiled. "What's your locus? Twentieth century? Twenty-first at the latest, I'd say."

"I'm from 1984. 1984 A.D."

Another smile, a self-satisfied one. "Not a bad guess, then." A brisk tilt of the head. "Y'ang-Yeovil."

"Pardon me?" Phillips said.

"Y'ang-Yeovil. It is my name. Formerly Colonel Y'ang-Yeovil of the Third Septentriad."

"Is that on some other planet?" asked Phillips, feeling a bit dazed.

"Oh, no, not at all," Y'ang-Yeovil said pleasantly. "This very world, I assure you. I am quite of human origin. Citizen of the Republic of Upper Han, native of the city of Port Ssu. And you—forgive me—your name—?"

"I'm sorry. Phillips. Charles Phillips. From New York City, once upon a time."

"Ah, New York!" Y'ang-Yeovil's face lit with a glimmer of recognition that quickly faded. "New York—New York—it was very famous, that I know—"

This is very strange, Phillips thought. He felt greater compassion for poor bewildered Francis Willoughby now. This man comes from a time so far beyond my own that he barely knows of New York—he must be a contemporary of the real New Chicago, in fact; I wonder whether he finds this version authentic—and yet to the citizens this Y'ang-Yeovil too is just a primitive, a curio out of antiquity—

"New York was the largest city of the United States of America," Phillips said.

"Of course. Yes. Very famous."

"But virtually forgotten by the time the Republic of Upper Han came into existence, I gather."

Y'ang-Yeovil said, looking uncomfortable, "There were disturbances between your time and mine. But by no means should you take from my words the impression that your city was—"

Sudden laughter resounded across the room. Five or six newcomers had arrived at the party. Phillips stared, gasped, gaped. Surely that was Stengard—and Aramayne beside him—and that other woman, half-hidden behind them—

"If you'll pardon me a moment—" Phillips said, turning abruptly away from Y'ang-Yeovil. "Please excuse me. Someone just coming in—a person I've been trying to find ever since—"

He hurried toward her.

"Gioia?" he called. "Gioia, it's me! Wait! Wait!"

Stengard was in the way. Aramayne, turning to take a handful of the little vapor-sniffers from Cantilena, blocked him also. Phillips pushed through them as though they were not there. Gioia, halfway out the door, halted and looked toward him like a frightened deer.

"Don't go," he said. He took her hand in his.

He was startled by her appearance. How long had it been since their strange parting on that night of mysteries in Chang-an? A year? A year and a half? So he believed. Or had he lost all track of time? Were his perceptions of the passing of the months in this world that unreliable? She seemed at least ten or fifteen years older. Maybe she really was; maybe the years had been passing for him here as in a dream, and he had never known it. She looked strained, faded, worn. Out of a thinner and strangely altered face her eyes blazed at him almost defiantly, as though saying, *See? See how ugly I have become?*

He said, "I've been hunting for you for—I

don't know how long it's been, Gioia. In Mohenjo, in Timbuctoo, now here. I want to be with you again."

"It isn't possible."

"Belilala explained everything to me in Mohenjo. I know that you're a short-timer—I know what that means, Gioia. But what of it? So you're beginning to age a little. So what? So you'll only have three or four hundred years, instead of forever. Don't you think I know what it means to be a short-timer? I'm just a simple ancient man of the twentieth century, remember? Sixty, seventy, eighty ears is all we would get. You and I suffer from the same malady, Gioia. That's what drew you to me in the first place. I'm certain of that. That's why we belong with each other now. However much time we have, we can spend the rest of it together, don't you see?"

"You're the one who doesn't see, Charles," she said softly.

"Maybe. Maybe I still don't understand a damned thing about this place. Except that you and I—that I love you—that I think you love me—"

"I love you, yes. But you don't understand. It's precisely because I love you that you and I—you and I can't—"

With a despairing sigh she slid her hand free of his grasp. He reached for her again, but she shook him off and backed up quickly into the corridor.

"Gioia?"

"Please," she said. "No. I would never have

come here if I knew you were here. Don't come after me. Please. Please."

She turned and fled.

He stood looking after her for a long moment. Cantilena and Aramayne appeared, and smiled at him as if nothing at all had happened. Cantilena offered him a vial of some sparking amber fluid. He refused with a brusque gesture. Where do I go now? he wondered. What do I do? He wandered back into the party.

Y'ang-Yeovil glided to his side. "You are in great distress," the little man murmured.

Phillips glared. "Let me be."

"Perhaps I could be of some help."

"There's no help possible," said Phillips. He swung about and plucked one of the vials from a tray and gulped its contents. It made him feel as if there were two of him, standing on either side of Y'ang-Yeovil. He gulped another. Now there were four of him. "I'm in love with a citizen," he blurted. It seemed to him that he was speaking in chorus.

"Love. Ah. And does she love you?"

"So I thought. So I think. But she's a short-timer. Do you know what that means? She's not immortal like the others. She ages. She's beginning to look old. And so she's been running away from me. She doesn't want me to see her changing. She thinks it'll disgust me, I suppose. I tried to remind her just now that I'm not immortal either, that she and I could grow old together, but she—"

"Oh, no," Y'ang-Yeovil said quietly. "Why do

you think you will age? Have you grown any older in all the time you have been here?"

Phillips was nonplussed. "Of course I have. I—I—"

"Have you?" Y'ang-Yeovil smiled. "Here. Look at yourself." He did something intricate with his fingers and a shimmering zone of mirror-like light appeared between them. Phillips stared at his reflection. A youthful face stared back at him. It was true, then. He had simply not thought about it. How many years had he spent in this world? The time had simply slipped by: a great deal of time, though he could not calculate how much. They did not seem to keep close count of it here, nor had he. But it must have been many years, he thought. All that endless travel up and down the globe—so many cities had come and gone— Rio, Rome, Asgard, those were the first three that came to mind—and there were others; he could hardly remember every one. Years. His face had not changed at all. Time had worked its harshness on Gioia, yes, but not on him.

"I don't understand," he said. "Why am I not aging?"

"Because you are not real," said Y'ang-Yeovil. "Are you unaware of that?"

Phillips blinked. "Not—real?"

"Did you think you were lifted bodily out of your own time?" the little man asked. "Ah, no, no, there is no way for them to do such a thing. We are not actual time travelers: not you, not I, not any of the visitors. I thought you were aware of that. But perhaps your era is too early for a proper understanding of these things. We are very cleverly done, my friend. We are ingenious constructs, marvelously stuffed with the thoughts and attitudes and events of our own times. We are their finest achievements, you know; far more complex even than one of these cities. We are a step beyond the temporaries—more than a step, a great deal more. They do only what they are instructed to do, and their range is very narrow. They are nothing but machines, really. Whereas we are autonomous. We move about by our own will; we think, we talk, we even, so it seems, fall in love. But we will not age. How could we age? We are not real. We are mere webworks of mental responses. We are mere illusions, done so well that we deceive even ourselves. You did not know that? Indeed, you did not know?"

He was airborne, touching destination buttons at random. Somehow he found himself heading back toward Timbuctoo. *This city is closed. This is not a place any longer.* It did not matter to him. Why should anything matter?

Fury and a choking sense of despair rose within him. I am software, Phillips thought. I am nothing but software.

Not real. Very cleverly done. An ingenious construct. A mere illusion.

No trace of Timbuctoo was visible from the air. He landed anyway. The gray sandy earth was smooth, unturned, as though there had never been anything there. A few robots were still about, handling whatever final chores were required in the shutting-down of a city. Two of them scuttled up to him. Huge bland gleaming silver-skinned insects, not friendly.

"There is no city here," they said. "This is not a permissible place."

"Permissible by whom?"

"There is no reason for you to be here."

"There's no reason for me to be anywhere," Phillips said. The robots stirred, made uneasy humming sounds and ominous clicks, waved their antennae about. They seemed troubled, he thought. They seem to dislike my attitude. Perhaps I run some risk of being taken off to the home for unruly software for debugging. "I'm leaving now," he told them. "Thank you. Thank you very much." He backed away from them and climbed into his flitterflitter. He touched more destination buttons.

We move about by our own will. We think, we talk, we even fall in love.

He landed in Chang-an. This time there was no reception committee waiting for him at the Gate of Brilliant Virtue. The city seemed larger and more resplendent: new pagodas, new palaces. It felt like winter: a chilly cutting wind was blowing. The sky was cloudless and dazzlingly bright. At the steps of the Silver Terrace he encountered Francis Willoughby, a great hulking figure in magnificent brocaded robes, with two dainty little temporaries, pretty as jade statuettes, engulfed in his arms. "Miracles and wonders! The silly lunatic fellow is here too!" Willoughby roared. "Look, look, we are come to far Cathay, you and I!"

We are nowhere, Phillips thought. *We are mere illusions, done so well that we deceive even ourselves.*

To Willoughby he said, "You look like an emperor in those robes, Francis."

"Aye, like Prester John!" Willoughby cried. "Like Tamburlaine himself! Aye, am I not majestic?" He slapped Phillips gaily on the shoulder, a rough playful poke that spun him halfway about, coughing and wheezing. "We flew in the air, as the eagles do, as the demons do, as the angels do! Soared like angels! Like angels!" He came close, looming over Phillips. "I would have gone to England, but the wench Belilala said there was an enchantment on me that would keep me from England just now; and so we voyaged to Cathay. Tell me this, fellow, will you go witness for me when we see England again? Swear that all that has befallen us did in truth befall? For I fear they will say I am as mad as Marco Polo, when I tell them of flying to Cathay."

"One madman backing another?" Phillips asked. "What can I tell you? You still think you'll reach England, do you?" Rage rose to the surface in him, bubbling hot. "Ah, Francis, Francis, do you know your Shakespeare? Did you go to the plays? We aren't real. *We aren't real.* We are such stuff as dreams are made on, the two of us. That's all we are. O brave new world! What England? Where? There's no England. There's no Francis Willoughby. There's no Charles Phillips. What we are is—"

"Let him be, Charles," a cool voice cut in.

He turned. Belilala, in the robes of an empress, was coming down the steps of the Silver Terrace.

"I know the truth," he said bitterly. "Y'ang-Yeovil told me. The visitor from the twenty-fifth century. I saw him in New Chicago."

"Did you see Gioia there too?" Belilala asked.

"Briefly. She looks much older."

"Yes. I know. She was here recently."

"And has gone on, I suppose?"

"To Mohenjo again, yes. Go after her, Charles. Leave poor Francis alone. I told her to wait for you. I told her that she needs you, and you need her."

"Very kind of you. But what good is it, Belilala? I don't even exist. And she's going to die."

"You exist. How can you doubt that you exist? You feel, don't you? You suffer. You love. You love Gioia: is that not so? And you are loved by Gioia. Would Gioia love what is not real?"

"You think she loves me?"

"I know she does. Go to her, Charles. Go. I told her to wait for you in Mohenjo."

Phillips nodded numbly. What was there to lose?

"Go to her," said Belilala again. "Now."

"Yes," Phillips said. "I'll go now." He turned to Willoughby. "If ever we meet in London, friend, I'll testify for you. Fear nothing. All will be well, Francis."

He left them and set his course for Mohenjo-daro, half expecting to find the robots already tearing it down. Mohenjo-daro was still there, no lovelier than before. He went to the baths, thinking he might find Gioia there. She was not; but he came upon Nissandra, Stengard, Fenimon. "She has gone to Alexandria," Fenimon told him. "She wants to see it one last time, before they close it."

"They're almost ready to open Constantinople," Stengard explained. "The capital of Byzantium, you know, the great city by the Golden Horn. They'll take Alexandria away, you understand, when Byzantium opens. They say it's going to be marvelous. We'll see you there for the opening, naturally?"

"Naturally," Phillips said.

He flew to Alexandria. He felt lost and weary. All this is hopeless folly, he told himself. I am nothing but a puppet jerking about on its strings. But somewhere above the shining breast of the Arabian sea the deeper implications of something that Belilala had said to him started to sink in, and he felt his bitterness, his rage, his despair, all suddenly beginning to leave him. *You exist. How can you doubt that you exist? Would Gioia love what is not real?* Of course. Of course. Y'ang-Yeovil had been wrong: visitors were something more than mere illusions. Indeed Y'ang-Yeovil had voiced the truth of their condition without understanding what he was really saying: *We think, we talk, we fall in love.* Yes. That was the heart of the situation. The visitors might be artificial, but they were not unreal. Belilala had been trying to tell him that just the other night. *You suffer. You love. You love Gioia. Would Gioia love what is not real?* Surely he was real, or at any rate real enough. What he was was something strange, something that would probably have been all but incomprehensible to the twentieth-century people whom he had been designed to simulate. But that did not mean that he was unreal. Did one have to be of woman born to be real? No. No. No. His kind of reality was a sufficient reality. He had no need to be ashamed of it. And, understanding that, he understood that Gioia did not need to grow old and die. There was a way by which she could be saved, if only she would embrace it. If only she would.

When he landed in Alexandria he went immediately to the hotel on the slopes of the Paneium where they had stayed on their first visit, so very long ago; and there she was, sitting quietly on a patio with a view of the harbor and the Lighthouse. There was something calm and resigned about the way she sat. She had given up. She did not even have the strength to flee from him any longer.

"Gioia," he said gently.

She looked older than she had in New Chicago. Her face was drawn and sallow and her eyes seemed sunken; and she was not even bothering these days to deal with the white strands that stood out in stark contrast against the darkness of her hair. He sat down beside her and put his hand over hers, and looked out toward the obelisks, the palaces, the temples, the Lighthouse. At length he said, "I know what I really am, now."

"Do you, Charles?" She sounded very far away.

"In my era we called it software. All I am is a set of commands, responses, cross-references, operating some sort of artificial body. It's infinitely better software than we could have imagined. But we were only just beginning to learn how, after all. They pumped me full of twentieth-century reflexes. The right moods, the right appetites, the right irrationalities, the right sort of combativeness. Somebody knows a lot about what it was like to be a twentieth-century man. They did a good job with Willoughby, too, all that Elizabethan rhetoric and swagger. And I suppose they got Y'ang-Yeovil right. *He* seems to think so: who better to judge? The twenty-fifth century, the Republic of Upper Han, people with gray-green skin, half Chinese and half Martian for all I know. *Somebody* knows. Somebody here is very good at programming, Gioia."

She was not looking at him.

"I feel frightened, Charles," she said in that same distant way.

"Of me? Of the things I'm saying?"

"No, not of you. Don't you see what has happened to me?"

"I see you. There are changes."

"I lived a long time wondering when the changes would begin. I thought maybe they wouldn't, not really. Who wants to believe they'll get old? But it started when we were in Alexandria that first time. In Chang-an it got much worse. And now—now—"

He said abruptly, "Stengard tells me they'll be opening Constantinople very soon."

"So?"

"Don't you want to be there when it opens?"

"I'm becoming old and ugly, Charles."

"We'll go to Constantinople together. We'll leave tomorrow, eh? What do you say? We'll charter a boat. It's a quick little hop, right across the Mediterranean. Sailing to Byzantium! There was a poem, you know, in my time. Not forgotten, I guess, because they've programmed it into me. All these thousands of years, and someone still remembers old Yeats. *The young in one another's arms, birds in the trees.* Come with me to Byzantium, Gioia."

She shrugged. "Looking like this? Getting more hideous every hour? While *they* stay young forever? While *you*—" She faltered; her voice cracked; she fell silent.

"Finish the sentence, Gioia."

"Please. Let me alone."

"You were going to say, 'While *you* stay young forever too, Charles,' isn't that it? You knew all along that I was never going to change. I didn't know that, but you did."

"Yes. I knew. I pretended that it wasn't true—that as I aged, you'd age too. It was very foolish of me. In Chang-an, when I first began to see the real signs of it—that was when I realized I couldn't stay with you any longer. Because I'd look at you, always young, always remaining the same age, and I'd look at myself, and—" She gestured, palms upward. "So I gave you to Belilala and ran away."

"All so unnecessary, Gioia."

"I didn't think it was."

"But you don't have to grow old. Not if you don't want to!"

"Don't be cruel, Charles," she said tonelessly. "There's no way of escaping what I have."

"But there is," he said.

"You know nothing about these things."

"Not very much, no," he said. "But I see how it can be done. Maybe it's a primitive simple-minded twentieth-century sort of solution, but I think it ought to work. I've been playing with the idea ever since I left Mohenjo. Tell me this, Gioia: Why can't you go to them, to the programmers, to the artificers, the planners, whoever they are, the ones who create the cities and the temporaries and the visitors. And have yourself made into something like me!"

She looked up, startled. "What are you saying?"

"They can cobble up a twentieth-century man out of nothing more than fragmentary records and make him plausible, can't they? Or an Elizabethan, or anyone else of any era at all, and he's authentic, he's convincing. So why couldn't they do an even better job with you? Produce a Gioia so real that even Gioia can't tell the difference? But a Gioia that will never age—a Gioia-construct, a Gioia-program, a visitor-Gioia! Why not? Tell me why not, Gioia."

She was trembling. "I've never heard of doing any such thing!"

"But don't you think it's possible?"

"How would I know?"

"Of course it's possible. If they can create visitors, they can take a citizen and duplicate her in such a way that—"

"It's never been done. I'm sure of it. I can't imagine any citizen agreeing to any such thing. To give up the body—to let yourself be turned into—into—"

She shook her head, but it seemed to be a gesture of astonishment as much as of negation.

He said, "Sure. To give up the body. Your natural body, your aging, shrinking, deteriorating short-timer body. What's so awful about that?"

She was very pale. "This is craziness, Charles. I don't want to talk about it any more."

"It doesn't sound crazy to me."

"You can't possibly understand."

"Can't I? I can certainly understand being afraid to die. I don't have a lot of trouble understanding what it's like to be one of the few aging people in a world where nobody grows old. What I can't understand is why you aren't even willing to consider the possibility that—"

"No," she said. "I tell you, it's crazy. They'd laugh at me."

"Who?"

"All of my friends. Hawk, Stengard, Aramayne—" Once again she would not look at him. "They can be very cruel, without even realizing it. They despise anything that seems ungraceful to them, anything sweaty and desperate and cowardly. Citizens don't do sweaty things, Charles. And that's how this will seem. Assuming it can be done at all. They'll be terribly patronizing. Oh, they'll be sweet to me, yes, dear Gioia, how wonderful for you, Gioia, but when I turn my back they'll laugh. They'll say the most wicked things about me. I couldn't bear that."

"They can afford to laugh," Phillips said. "It's easy to be brave and cool about dying when you know you're going to live forever. How very fine for them; but why should you be the only one to grow old and die? And they won't laugh, anyway. They're not as cruel as you think. Shallow, maybe, but not cruel. They'll be glad that you've found a way to save yourself. At the very least, they won't have to feel guilty about you any longer, and that's bound to please them. You can—"

"Stop it," she said.

She rose, walked to the railing of the patio, stared out toward the sea. He came up behind her. Red sails in the harbor, sunlight glittering along the sides of the Lighthouse, the palaces of the Ptolemies stark white against the sky. Lightly he rested his hand on her shoulder. She twitched as if to pull away from him, but remained where she was.

"Then I have another idea," he said quietly. "If you won't go to the planners, *I* will. Reprogram me, I'll say. Fix things so that I start to age at the same rate you do. I'll be more authentic, anyway, if I'm supposed to be playing the part of a twentieth-century man. Over the years I'll very gradually get some lines in my face, my hair will turn gray, I'll walk a little more slowly—we'll grow old together, Gioia. To hell with your lovely immortal friends. We'll have each other. We won't need them."

She swung around. Her eyes were wide with horror.

"Are you serious, Charles?"

"Of course."

"No," she murmured. "No. Everything you've said to me today is monstrous nonsense. Don't you realize that?"

He reached for her hand and enclosed her fingertips in his. "All I'm trying to do is find some way for you and me to—"

"Don't say any more," she said. "Please." Quickly, as though drawing back from a suddenly flaring flame, she tugged her fingers free of his and put her hand behind her. Though his face was just inches from hers he felt an immense chasm opening between them. They stared at one another for a moment; then she moved deftly to his left, darted around him, and ran from the patio.

Stunned, he watched her go, down the long marble corridor and out of sight. It was folly to give pursuit, he thought. She was lost to him: that was clear, that was beyond any question. She was terrified of him. Why cause her even more anguish? But somehow he found himself running through the halls of the hotel, along the winding garden path, into the cool green groves of the Paneium. He thought he saw her on the portico of Hadrian's palace, but when he got there the echoing stone halls were empty. To a temporary that was sweeping the steps he said, "Did you see a woman come this way?" A blank sullen stare was his only answer.

Phillips cursed and turned away.

"Gioia?" he called. "Wait! Come back!"

Was that her, going into the Library? He rushed past the startled mumbling librarians and sped through the stacks, peering beyond the mounds of double-handled scrolls into the shadowy corridors. "Gioia? *Gioia!*" It was a desecration, bellowing like that in this quiet place. He scarcely cared.

Emerging by a side door, he loped down to the harbor. The Lighthouse! Terror enfolded him. She might already be a hundred steps up that ramp, heading for the parapet from which she meant to fling herself into the sea. Scattering citizens and temporaries as if they were straws, he ran within. Up he went, never pausing for breath, though his synthetic lungs were screaming for respite, his ingeniously designed heart was desperately pounding. On the first balcony he imagined he caught a glimpse of her, but he circled it without finding her.

Onward, upward. He went to the top, to the
beacon chamber itself: no Gioia. Had she
jumped? Had she gone down one ramp while
he was ascending the other? He clung to the
rim and looked out, down, searching the base
of the Lighthouse, the rocks offshore, the
causeway. No Gioia. I will find her somewhere, he thought. I will keep going until I find
her. He went running down the ramp, calling
her name. He reached ground level and
sprinted back toward the center of town.
Where next? The temple of Poseidon? The
tomb of Cleopatra?

He paused in the middle of Canopus Street,
groggy and dazed.

"Charles?" she said.

"Where are you?"

"Right here. Beside you." She seemed to ma-
terialize from the air. Her face was unflushed,
her robe bore no trace of perspiration. Had he
been chasing a phantom through the city? She
came to him and took his hand, and said softly,
tenderly, "Were your really serious, about
having them make you age?"

"If there's no other way, yes."

"The other way is so frightening, Charles."

"Is it?"

"You can't understand how much."

"More frightening than growing old? Than
dying?"

"I don't know," she said. "I suppose not. The
only thing I'm sure of is that I don't want you
to get old, Charles."

"But I won't have to. Will I?" He stared at her.

"No," she said. "You won't have to. Neither of us will."

Phillips smiled. "We should get away from here," he said after a while. "Let's go across to Byzantium, yes, Gioia? We'll show up in Constantinople for the opening. Your friends will be there. We'll tell them what you've decided to do. They'll know how to arrange it. Someone will."

"It sounds so strange," said Gioia. "To turn myself into—into a visitor? A visitor in my own world?"

"That's what you've always been, though."

"I suppose. In a way. But at least I've been *real* up to now."

"Whereas I'm not?"

"Are you, Charles?"

"Yes. Just as real as you. I was angry at first, when I found out the truth about myself. But I came to accept it. Somewhere between Mohenjo and here, I came to see that it was all right to be what I am: that I perceive things, I form ideas, I draw conclusions. I am very well designed, Gioia. I can't tell the difference between being what I am and being completely alive, and to me that's being real enough. I think, I feel, I experience joy and pain. I'm as real as I need to be. And you will be too. You'll never stop being Gioia, you know. It's only your body that you'll cast away, the body that played such a terrible joke on you anyway."

He brushed her cheek with his hand. "It was all said for us before, long ago:

"*Once out of nature I shall never take*
My bodily form from any natural thing,
But such a form as Grecian goldsmiths make
of hammered gold and gold enamelling
To keep a drowsy Emperor awake—"

"Is that the same poem?" she asked.

"The same poem, yes. The ancient poem that isn't quite forgotten yet."

"Finish it, Charles."

—"*Or set upon a golden bough to sing*
To lords and ladies of Byzantium
Of what is past, or passing, or to come."

"How beautiful. What does it mean?"

"That it isn't necessary to be mortal. That we can allow ourselves to be gathered into the artifice of eternity, that we can be transformed, that we can move on beyond the flesh. Yeats didn't mean it in quite the way I do—he wouldn't have begun to comprehend what we're talking about, not a word of it—and yet, and yet—the underlying truth is the same. Live, Gioia! With me!" He turned to her and saw color coming into her pallid cheeks. "It does make sense, what I'm suggesting, doesn't it? You'll attempt it, won't you? Whoever makes the visitors can be induced to remake you. Right? What do you think: can they, Gioia?"

She nodded in a barely perceptible way. "I think so," she said faintly. "It's very strange. But I think it ought to be possible. Why not, Charles? Why not?"

"Yes," he said. "Why not?"

In the morning they hired a vessel in the harbor, a low sleek pirogue with a blood-red sail, skippered by a rascally-looking temporary whose smile was irresistible. Phillips shaded his eyes and peered northward across the sea. He thought he could almost make out the shape of the great city sprawling on its seven hills, Constantine's New Rome beside the Golden Horn, the mighty dome of Hagia Sophia, the somber walls of the citadel, the palaces and churches, the Hippodrome, Christ in glory rising above all else in brilliant mosaic streaming with light.

"Byzantium," Phillips said. "Take us there the shortest and quickest way."

"It is my pleasure," said the boatman with unexpected grace.

Gioia smiled. He had not seen her looking so vibrantly alive since the night of the imperial feast in Chang-an. He reached for her hand—her slender fingers were quivering lightly—and helped her into the boat.

THE TOR DOUBLES

Tor is proud to bring you the best in science fiction's short novels. An amazing amount of particularly fine science fiction is written at a length just too short to put in a book by itself, so we're providing them two at a time.

The Tor Doubles will be both new stories and older ones, all carefully chosen. Whichever side you start with, you will be able to turn the book over and enjoy the other side just as much.

The first impression one gets of America is that it is not as poor as one has been told. It is only later that it becomes apparent how much has been handed down from the previous century. The streets here are paved, but they are old and broken. There are fine, though decayed, buildings everywhere (this hotel is one—the Inn of Holidays, it is called), more modern in appearance than the ones we see at home.

I asked the manager where I should go to see the sights of the city. "There are no tours," he said. "Not any more."

I set off for the north when I left the hotel. What American cities might be like if these people thronged the streets then, I cannot imagine. Even by clearest day, there is the impression of a carnival, of some mad circus whose performance began a hundred or more years ago and has not ended yet.

The Tor Double Novels

*forthcoming

GENE WOLFE

SEVEN AMERICAN NIGHTS

TOR®

A TOM DOHERTY ASSOCIATES BOOK
NEW YORK

This is a work of fiction. All the characters and events portrayed in this book are fictitious, and any resemblance to real people or events is purely coincidental.

SEVEN AMERICAN NIGHTS

Copyright © 1978 by Gene Wolfe

All rights reserved, including the right to reproduce this book or portions thereof in any form.

A TOR Book
Published by Tom Doherty Associates, Inc.
49 West 24 Street
New York, NY 10010

Cover art by Bryn Barnard

ISBN: 0-812-50079-2   Can. ISBN: 0-812-55924-X

First Tor edition: July 1989

Printed in the United States of America

0 9 8 7 6 5 4 3 2 1

ESTEEMED AND LEARNED MADAME:

As I last wrote you, it appears to me likely
that your son Nadan (may Allah preserve
him!) has left the old capital and traveled—of his own will or another's—north
into the region about the Bay of Delaware.
My conjecture is now confirmed by the
discovery in those regions of the notebook
I enclose. It is not of American manufacture, as you see; and though it holds only
the records of a single week, several sug-
gestive items therein provide us new reason to hope.

I have photocopied the contents to guide
me in my investigations; but I am alert to
the probability that you, madame, with
your superior knowledge of the young
man we seek, may discover implications I
have overlooked. Should that be the case,
I urge you to write me at once.

Though I hesitate to mention it in con-
nection with so encouraging a finding,
your most recently due remission has not

yet arrived. I assume that this tardiness results from the procrastination of the mails, which is here truly abominable. I must warn you, however, that I shall be forced to discontinue the search unless funds sufficient for my expenses are forthcoming before the advent of winter.

With inexpressible respect,
HASSAN KERBELAI

Here I am at last! After twelve mortal days aboard the *Princess Fatimah*—twelve days of cold and ennui—twelve days of bad food and throbbing engines—the joy of being on land again is like the delight a condemned man must feel when a letter from the shah snatches him from beneath the very blade of death. America! America! Dull days are no more! They say that everyone who comes here either loves or hates you, America—by Allah I love you now!

Having begun this record at last, I find I do not know where to begin. I had been reading travel diaries before I left home; and so when I saw you, O Book, lying so square and thick in your stall in the bazaar—why should I not have adventures too, and write a book like Osman Aga's? Few come to this sad country at the world's edge, after all, and most who do land farther up the coast.

And that gives me the clue I was looking for—how to begin. America began for me as colored water. When I went out on deck yesterday morning, the ocean had changed from

green to yellow. I had never heard of such a thing before, neither in my reading, nor in my talks with Uncle Mirza, who was here thirty years ago. I am afraid I behaved like the greatest fool imaginable, running about the ship babbling, and looking over the side every few minutes to make certain the rich mustard color was still there and would not vanish the way things do in dreams when we try to point them out to someone else. The steward told me he knew. Golam Gassem the grain merchant (whom I had tried to avoid meeting for the entire trip until that moment) said, "Yes, yes," and turned away in a fashion that showed he had been avoiding me too, and that it was going to take more of a miracle than yellow water to change his feelings.

One of the few native Americans in first class came out just then: Mister—as the style is here—Tallman, husband of the lovely Madam Tallman, who really deserves such a tall man as myself. (Whether her husband chose that name in self-derision, or in the hope that it would erase others' memory of his infirmity; or whether it was his father's, and is merely one of the countless ironies of fate, I do not know. There was something wrong with his back.) As if I had not made enough spectacle of myself already, I took this Mr. Tallman by the sleeve and told him to look over the side, explaining that the sea had turned yellow. I am afraid Mr. Tallman turned white himself instead, and turned something else too—his back—looking as though he would have struck

me if he dared. It was comic enough, I suppose—I heard some of the other passengers chuckling about it afterward—but I don't believe I have seen such hatred in a human face before. Just then the captain came strolling up, and I—considerably deflated but not flattened yet, and thinking that he had not overheard Mr. Tallman and me—mentioned for the final time that day that the water had turned yellow. "I know," the captain said. "It's his country" (here he jerked his head in the direction of the pitiful Mr. Tallman), "bleeding to death."

Here it is evening again, and I see that I stopped writing last night before I had so much as described my first sight of the coast. Well, so be it. At home it is midnight, or nearly, and the life of the cafés is at its height. How I wish that I were there now, with you, Yasmin, not webbed among these red- and purple-clad strangers, who mob their own streets like an invading army, and duck into their houses like rats into their holes. But you, Yasmin, or Mother, or whoever may read this, will want to know of *my* day—only you are sometimes to think of me as I am now, bent over an old scarred table in a decayed room with two beds, listening to the hastening feet in the streets outside.

I slept late this morning; I suppose I was more tired from the voyage than I realized. By the time I woke, the whole of the city was alive around me, with vendors crying fish and fruits

under my shuttered window, and the great wooden wains the Americans call *trucks* rumbling over the broken concrete on their wide iron wheels, bringing up goods from the shops in the Potomac anchorage. One sees very odd teams here, Yasmin. When I went to get my breakfast (one must go outside to reach the lobby and dining room in these American hotels, which I would think would be very inconvenient in bad weather) I saw one of these *trucks* with two oxen, a horse, and a mule in the traces, which would have made you laugh. The drivers crack their whips all the time.

The first impression one gets of America is that it is not as poor as one has been told. It is only later that it becomes apparent how much has been handed down from the previous century. The streets here are paved, but they are old and broken. There are fine, though decayed, buildings everywhere (this hotel is one—the Inn of Holidays, it is called), more modern in appearance than the ones we see at home, where for so long traditional architecture was enforced by law. We are on Maine Street, and when I had finished my breakfast (it was very good, and very cheap by our standards, though I am told it is impossible to get anything out of season here) I asked the manager where I should go to see the sights of the city. He is a short and phenomenally ugly man, something of a hunchback as so many of them are. "There are not tours," he said. "Not any more."

I told him that I simply wanted to wander about myself, and perhaps sketch a bit.

"You can do that. North for the buildings, south for the theater, west for the park. Do you plan to go to the park, Mr. Jaffarzadeh?"

"I haven't decided yet."

"You should hire at least two securities if you go to the park—I can recommend an agency."

"I have my pistol."

"You'll need more than that, sir."

Naturally, I decided then and there that I would go to the park, and alone. But I have determined not to spend this, the sole, small coin of adventure this land has provided me so far, before I discover what else it may offer to enrich my existence.

Accordingly, I set off for the north when I left the hotel. I have not, thus far, seen this city, or any American city, by night. What they might be like if these people thronged the streets then, as we do, I cannot imagine. Even by clearest day, there is the impression of a carnival, of some mad circus whose performance began a hundred or more years ago and has not ended yet.

At first it seemed that only every fourth or fifth person suffered some trace of the genetic damage that destroyed the old America, but as I grew more accustomed to the streets, and thus less quick to dismiss as Americans and no more the unhappy old woman who wanted me to buy flowers and the boy who dashed shrieking between the wheels of a *truck*, and

began instead to look at them as human beings—in other words, just as I would look at some chance-met person on one of our own streets—I saw that there was hardly a soul not marked in some way. These deformities, though they are individually hideous, in combination with the bright, ragged clothing so common here, give the meanest assemblage the character of a pageant. I sauntered along, hardly out of earshot of one group of street musicians before encountering another, and in a few strides passed a man so tall that he was taller seated on a low step than I standing; a bearded dwarf with a withered arm; and a woman whose face had been divided by some devil into halves, one large-eyed and idiotically despairing, the other squinting and sneering.

There can be no question about it—Yasmin must not read this. I have been sitting here for an hour at least, staring at the flame of the candle. Sitting and listening to something that from time to time beats against the steel shutters that close the window of this room. The truth is that I am paralyzed by a fear that entered me—I do not know from whence—yesterday, and has been growing ever since.

Everyone knows that these Americans were once the most skilled creators of consciousness-altering substances the world has ever seen. The same knowledge that permitted them to forge the chemicals that destroyed them (so that they might have bread that never staled, innumerable poi-

sons for vermin, and a host of unnatural materials for every purpose) also contrived synthetic alkaloids that produced endless feverish imaginings.

Surely some, at least, of these skills remain. Or if they do not, then some of the substances themselves, preserved for eighty or a hundred years in hidden cabinets, and no doubt growing more dangerous as the world forgets them. I think that someone on the ship may have administered some such drug to me.

That is out at last! I felt so much better at having written it—it took a great deal of effort—that I took several turns about this room. Now that I have written it down, I do not believe it at all.

Still, last night I dreamed of that bread, of which I first read in the little schoolroom of Uncle Mirza's country house. It was no complex, towering "literary" dream such as I have sometimes had, and embroidered, and boasted of afterward over coffee. Just the vision of a loaf of soft white bread lying on a plate in the center of a small table: bread that retained the fragrance of the oven (surely one of the most delicious in the world) though it was smeared with gray mold. Why would the Americans wish such a thing? Yet all the historians agree that they did, just as they wished their own corpses to appear living forever.

It is only this country, with its colorful, fetid streets, deformed people, and harsh, alien language, that makes me feel as drugged and

dreaming as I do. Praise Allah that I can speak Farsi to you, O Book. Will you believe that I have taken out every article of clothing I have, just to read the makers' labels? Will *I* believe it, for that matter, when I read this at home?

The public buildings to the north—once the great center, as I understand it, of political activity—offer a severe contrast to the streets of the still-occupied areas. In the latter, the old buildings are in the last stages of decay, or have been repaired by makeshift and inappropriate means; but they seethe with the life of those who depend upon such commercial activity as the port yet provides, and with those who depend on them, and so on. The monumental buildings, because they were constructed of the most imperishable materials, appear almost whole, though there are a few fallen columns and sagging porticos, and in several places small trees (mostly the sad *carpinus caroliniana*, I believe) have rooted in the crevices of walls. Still, if it is true, as has been written, that Time's beard is gray not with the passage of years but with the dust of ruined cities, it is here that he trails it. These imposing shells are no more than that. They were built, it would seem, to be cooled and ventilated by machinery. Many are windowless, their interiors now no more than sunless caves, reeking of decay; into these I did not venture. Others had had fixed windows that once were mere walls of glass; and a few of these remained, so that I was able to sketch

their construction. Most, however, are destroyed. Time's beard has swept away their very shards.

Though these old buildings (with one or two exceptions) are deserted, I encountered several beggars. They seemed to be Americans whose deformities preclude their doing useful work, and one cannot help but feel sorry for them, though their appearance is often as distasteful as their importunities. They offered to show me the former residence of their Padshah, and as an excuse to give them a few coins I accompanied them, making them first pledge to leave me when I had seen it.

The structure they pointed out to me was situated at the end of a long avenue lined with impressive buildings; so I suppose they must have been correct in thinking it once important. Hardly more than the foundation, some rubble, and one ruined wing remain now, and it cannot have been originally of an enduring construction. No doubt it was actually a summer palace or something of that kind. The beggars have now forgotten its very name, and call it merely "the white house."

When they had guided me to this relic, I pretended that I wanted to make drawings, and they left as they had promised. In five or ten minutes, however, one particularly enterprising fellow returned. He had no lower jaw, so that I had quite a bit of difficulty in understanding him at first; but after we had shouted back and forth a good deal—I telling him to depart and threatening to kill him on the spot,

and he protesting—I realized that he was forced to make the sound of *d* for *b*, *n* for *m*, and *t* for *p*; and after that we got along better.

I will not attempt to render his speech phonetically, but he said that since I had been so generous, he wished to show me a great secret—something foreigners like myself did not even realize existed.

"Clean water," I suggested.

"No, no. A great, great secret, Captain. You think all this is dead." He waved a misshapen hand at the desolated structures that surrounded us.

"Indeed I do."

"One still lives. You would like to see it? I will guide. Don't worry about the others— they're afraid of me. I will drive them away."

"If you are leading me into some kind of ambush, I warn you, you will be the first to suffer."

He looked at me very seriously for a moment, and a man seemed to stare from the eyes in that ruined face, so that I felt a twinge of real sympathy. "See there? The big building to the south, on Pennsylvania? Captain, my father's father's father was chief of a department ('detartnent') there. I would not betray you."

From what I have read of this country's policies in the days of his father's father's father, that was little enough reassurance, but I followed him.

We went diagonally across several blocks, passing through two ruined buildings. There were human bones in both, and remembering

his boast, I asked him if they had belonged to the workers there.

"No, no." He tapped his chest again—a habitual gesture, I suppose—and scooping up a skull from the floor held it beside his own head so that I could see that it exhibited cranial deformities much like his own. "We sleep here, to be shut behind strong walls from the things that come at night. We die here, mostly in wintertime. No one buries us."

"You should bury each other," I said.

He tossed down the skull, which shattered on the terrazzo floor, waking a thousand dismal echoes. "No shovel, and few are strong. But come with me."

At first sight the building to which he led me looked more decayed than many of the ruins. One of its spires had fallen, and the bricks lay in the street. Yet when I looked again, I saw that there must be something in what he said. The broken windows had been closed with ironwork at least as well made as the shutters that protect my room here; and the door, though old and weathered, was tightly shut, and looked strong.

"This is the museum," my guide told me. "The only part left, almost, of the Silent City that still lives in the old way. Would you like to see inside?"

I told him that I doubted that we would be able to enter.

"Wonderful machines." He pulled at my sleeve. "You *see* in, Captain. Come."

We followed the building's walls around sev-

eral corners, and at last entered a sort of alcove at the rear. Here there was a grill set in the weed-grown ground, and the beggar gestured toward it proudly. I made him stand some distance off, then knelt as he had indicated to look through the grill.

There was a window of unshattered glass beyond the grill. It was very soiled now, but I could see through into the basement of the building, and there, just as the beggar had said, stood an orderly array of complex mechanisms.

I stared for some time, trying to gain some notion of their purpose; and at length an old American appeared among them, peering at one and then another, and whisking the shining bars and gears with a rag.

The beggar had crept closer as I watched. He pointed at the old man, and said, "Still come from north and south to study here. Someday we are great again." Then I thought of my own lovely country, whose eclipse—though without genetic damage—lasted twenty-three hundred years. And I gave him money, and told him that, yes, I was certain America would be great again someday, and left him, and returned here.

I have opened the shutters so that I can look across the city to the obelisk and catch the light of the dying sun. Its fields and valleys of fire do not seem more alien to me, or more threatening, than this strange, despondent land. Yet I know that we are all one—the beggar, the old man moving among the machines

of a dead age, those machines themselves, the sun, and I. A century ago, when this was a thriving city, the philosophers used to speculate on the reason that each neutron and proton and electron exhibited the same mass as all the others of its kind. Now we know that there is only one particle of each variety, moving backward and forward in time, an electron when it travels as we do, a positron when its temporal displacement is retrograde, the same few particles appearing billions of billions of times to make up a single object, and the same few particles forming all the objects, so that we are all the sketches, as it were, of the same set of pastels.

I have gone out to eat. There is a good restaurant not far from the hotel, better even than the dining room here. When I came back the manager told me that there is to be a play tonight at the theater, and assured me that because it is so close to his hotel (in truth, he is very proud of this theater, and no doubt its proximity to his hotel is the only circumstance that permits the hotel to remain open) I will be in no danger if I go without an escort. To tell the truth, I am a little ashamed that I did not hire a boat today to take me across the channel to the park; so now I will attend the play, and dare the night streets.

Here I am again, returned to this too-large, too-bare, uncarpeted room, which is already beginning to seem a second home, with no adventures to retail from the dangerous be-

nighted streets. The truth is that the theater is hardly more than a hundred paces to the south. I kept my hand on the butt of my pistol and walked along with a great many other people (mostly Americans) who were also going to the theater, and felt something of a fool.

The building is as old as those in the Silent City, I should think; but it has been kept in some repair. There was more of a feeling of gaiety (though to me it was largely an alien gaiety) among the audience than we have at home, and less of the atmosphere of what I may call the sacredness of Art. By that I knew that the drama really is sacred here, as the colorful clothes of the populace make clear in any case. An exaggerated and solemn respect always indicates a loss of faith.

Having recently come from my dinner, I ignored the stands in the lobby at which the Americans—who seem to eat constantly when they can afford it—were selecting various cold meats and pastries, and took my place in the theater proper. I was hardly in my seat before a pipe-puffing old gentleman, an American, desired me to move in order that he might reach his own. I stood up gladly, of course, and greeted him as "Grandfather," as our own politeness (if not theirs) demands. But while he was settling himself and I was still standing beside him, I caught a glimpse of his face from the exact angle at which I had seen it this afternoon, and recognized him as the old man I had watched through the grill.

Here was a difficult situation. I wanted very

much to draw him into conversation, but I could not well confess that I had been spying on him. I puzzled over the question until the lights were extinguished and the play began.

It was Vidal's *Visit to a Small Planet*, one of the classics of the old American theater, a play I have often read about but never (until now) seen performed. I would have liked it much better if it had been done with the costumes and settings of its proper period; unhappily, the director had chosen to "modernize" the entire affair, just as we sometimes present *Rustam Beg* as if Rustam had been a hero of the war just past. General Powers was a contemporary American soldier with the mannerisms of a cowardly bandit; Spelding, a publisher of libelous broadsheets, and so on. The only characters that gave me much pleasure were the limping spaceman, Kreton, and the ingenue, Ellen Spelding, played as and by a radiantly beautiful American blonde.

All through the first act my mind had been returning (particularly during Spelding's speeches) to the problem of the old man beside me. By the time the curtain fell, I had decided that the best way to start a conversation might be to offer to fetch him a kebab—or whatever he might want—from the lobby, since his thread-bare appearance suggested that he might be ready enough to be treated, and the weakness of his legs would provide an admirable excuse. I tried the gambit as soon as the flambeaux were relit, and it worked as well as I could have wished. When I returned with a

paper tray of sandwiches and bitter drinks, he remarked to me quite spontaneously that he had noticed me flexing my right hand during the performance.

"Yes," I said, "I had been writing a good deal before I came here."

That set him off, and he began to discourse, frequently with a great deal more detail than I could comprehend, on the topic of writing machines. At last I halted the flow with some question that must have revealed that I knew less of the subject than he had supposed. "Have you ever," he asked me, "carved a letter in a potato, and moistened it with a stamp pad, and used it to imprint paper?"

"As a child, yes. We use a turnip, but no doubt the principle is the same."

"Exactly; and the principle is that of extended abstraction. I ask you—on the lowest level, what is communication?"

"Talking, I suppose."

His shrill laugh rose above the hubbub of the audience. "Not at all! Smell (here he gripped my arm), "smell is the essence of communication. Look at that word *essence* itself. When you smell another human being, you take chemicals from his body into your own, analyze them, and from the analysis you accurately deduce his emotional state. You do it so constantly and so automatically that you are largely unconscious of it, and say simply, 'He seemed frightened,' or 'He was angry.' You see?"

I nodded, interested in spite of myself.

"When you speak, you are telling another how you would smell if you smelled as you should and if he could smell you properly from where he stands. It is almost certain that speech was not developed until the glaciations that terminated the Pliocene stimulated mankind to develop fire, and the frequent inhalation of wood smoke had dulled the olfactory organs."

"I see."

"No; you hear—unless you are by chance reading my lips, which in this din would be a useful accomplishment." He took an enormous bite of his sandwich, spilling pink meat that had surely come from no natural animal. "When you write, you are telling the other how you would speak if he could hear you, and when you print with your turnip, you are telling him how you would write. You will notice that we have already reached the third level of abstraction."

I nodded again.

"It used to be believed that only a limited number K of levels of abstraction were possible before the original matter disappeared altogether—some very interesting mathematical work was done about seventy years ago in an attempt to derive a generalized expression for K for various systems. Now we know that the number can be infinite if the array represents an open curve, and that closed curves are also possible."

"I don't understand."

"You are young and handsome—very fine

looking, with your wide shoulders and black mustache; let us suppose a young woman loves you. If you and I and she were crouched now on the limb of a tree, you would scent her desire. Today, perhaps she tells you of that desire. But it is also possible, is it not, that she may write you of her desire?"

Remembering Yasmin's letters, I assented.

"But suppose those letters are perfumed—a musky, sweet perfume. You understand? A closed curve—the perfume is not the odor of her body, but an artificial simulation of it. It may not be what she feels, but it is what she tells you she feels. Your real love is for a whale, a male deer, and a bed of roses." He was about to say more, but the curtain went up for the second act.

I found that act both more enjoyable, and more painful, than the first. The opening scene, in which Kreton (soon joined by Ellen) reads the mind of the family cat, was exceptionally effective. The concealed orchestra furnished music to indicate cat thoughts; I wish I knew the identity of the composer, but my playbill does not provide the information. The bedroom wall became a shadow screen, where we saw silhouettes of cats catching birds, and then, when Ellen tickled the real cat's belly, making love. As I have said, Kreton and Ellen were the play's best characters. The juxtaposition of Ellen's willowy beauty and high-spirited naiveté, and Kreton's clear desire for her, illuminated perfectly the Paphian difficul-

ties that would confront a powerful telepath, were such persons to exist.

On the other hand, Kreton's summoning of the presidents, which closes the act, was as objectionable as it could possibly have been made. The foreign ruler conjured up by error was played as a Turk, and as broadly as possible. I confess to feeling some prejudice against that bloodthirsty race myself, but what was done was indefensible. When the president of the World Council appeared, he was portrayed as an American.

By the end of that scene I was in no very good mood. I think that I have not yet shaken off the fatigues of the crossing; and they, combined with a fairly strenuous day spent prowling around the ruins of the Silent City, had left me now in that state in which the smallest irritation takes on the dimensions of a mortal insult. The old curator beside me discerned my irascibility, but mistook the reason for it, and began to apologize for the state of the American stage, saying that all the performers of talent emigrated as soon as they gained recognition, and returned only when they had failed on the eastern shore of the Atlantic.

"No, no," I said. "Kreton and the girl are very fine, and the rest of the cast is at least adequate."

He seemed not to have heard me. "They pick them up wherever they can—they choose them for their faces. When they have appeared in three plays, they call themselves actors. At the Smithsonian—I am employed there, perhaps

I've already mentioned it—we have tapes of real theater: Laurence Olivier, Orson Welles, Katharine Cornell. Spelding is a barber, or at least he was. He used to put his chair under the old Kennedy statue and shave the passersby. Ellen is a trollop, and Powers a drayman. That lame fellow Kreton used to snare sailors for a singing house on Portland Street."

His disparagement of his own national culture embarrassed me, though it put me in a better mood. (I have noticed that the two often go together—perhaps I am secretly humiliated to find that people of no great importance can affect my interior state with a few words or some mean service.) I took my leave of him and went to the confectioner's stand in the lobby. The Americans have a very pretty custom of duplicating the speckled eggs of wild birds in marzipan, and I bought a box of these—not only because I wanted to try them myself, but because I felt certain they would prove a treat for the old man, who must seldom have enough money to afford luxuries of that kind. I was quite correct—he ate them eagerly. But when I sampled one, I found its odor (as though I were eating artificial violets) so unpleasant that I did not take another.

"We were speaking of writing," the old man said. "The closed curve and the open curve. I did not have time to make the point that both could be achieved mechanically; but the monograph I am now developing turns upon that very question, and it happens that I have examples with me. First the closed curve. In the

days when our president was among the
world's ten most powerful men—the reality of
the Paul Laurent you see on the stage there—
each president received hundreds of requests
every day for his signature. To have granted
them would have taken hours of his time. To
have refused them would have raised a bri-
gade of enemies."

"What did they do?"

"They called upon the resources of science.
That science devised the machine that wrote
this."

From within his clean, worn coat he drew a
folded sheet of paper. I opened it and saw that
it was covered with the text of what appeared
to be a public address, written in a childish
scrawl. Mentally attempting to review the list
of the American presidents I had seen in some
digest of world history long ago, I asked whose
hand it was.

"The machine's. Whose hand is being imi-
tated here is one of the things I am attempting
to discover."

In the dim light of the theater it was almost
impossible to make out the faded script, but I
caught the word *Sardinia*. "Surely, by corre-
lating the contents to historical events it
should be possible to date it quite accurately."

The old man shook his head. "The text itself
was composed by another machine to achieve
some national psychological effect. It is not
probable that it bears any real relationship to
the issues of its day. But now look here." He
drew out a second sheet, and unfolded it for

me. So far as I could see, it was completely blank. I was still staring at it when the curtain went up.

As Kreton moved his toy aircraft across the stage, the old man took a final egg and turned away to watch the play. There was still half a carton left, and I, thinking that he might want more later, and afraid that they might be spilled from my lap and lost underfoot, closed the box and slipped it into the side pocket of my jacket.

The special effects for the landing of the second spaceship were well done; but there was something else in the third act that gave me as much pleasure as the cat scene in the second. The final curtain hinges on the device our poets call the *Peri's asphodel*, a trick so shopworn now that it is acceptable only if it can be presented in some new light. The one used here was to have John—Ellen's lover—find Kreton's handkerchief and, remarking that it seemed perfumed, bury his nose in it. For an instant, the shadow wall used at the beginning of the second act was illuminated again to graphically (or I should say, pornographically) present Ellen's desire, conveying to the audience that John had, for that moment, shared the telepathic abilities of Kreton, whom all of them had now entirely forgotten.

The device was extremely effective, and left me feeling that I had by no means wasted my evening. I joined the general applause as the cast appeared to take their bows; then, as I

was turning to leave, I noticed that the old man appeared very ill. I asked if he were all right, and he confessed ruefully that he had eaten too much, and thanked me again for my kindness—which must at that time have taken a great deal of resolution.

I helped him out of the theater, and when I saw that he had no transportation but his feet, told him I would take him home. He thanked me again, and informed me that he had a room at the museum.

Thus the half-block walk from the theater to my hotel was transformed into a journey of three or four kilometers, taken by moonlight, much of it through rubble-strewn avenues of the deserted parts of the city.

During the day I had hardly glanced at the stark skeleton of the old highway. Tonight, when we walked beneath its ruined overpasses, they seemed inexpressibly ancient and sinister. It occurred to me then that there may be a time-flaw, such as astronomers report from space, somewhere in the Atlantic. How is it that this western shore is more antiquated in the remains of a civilization not yet a century dead than we are in the shadow of Darius? May it not be that every ship that plows that sea moves through ten thousand years?

For the past hour—I find I cannot sleep—I have been debating whether to make this entry. But what good is a travel journal, if one does not enter everything? I will revise it on

the trip home, and present a cleansed copy for my mother and Yasmin to read.

It appears that the scholars at the museum have no income but that derived from the sale of treasures gleaned from the past; and I bought a vial of what is supposed to be the greatest creation of the old hallucinatory chemists from the woman who helped me get the old man into bed. It is—it was—about half the height of my smallest finger. Very probably it was alcohol and nothing more, though I paid a substantial price.

I was sorry I had bought it before I left, and still more sorry when I arrived here; but at the time it seemed that this would be my only opportunity, and I could think of nothing but to seize the adventure. After I have swallowed the drug I will be able to speak with authority about these things for the remainder of my life.

Here is what I have done. I have soaked the porous sugar of one of the eggs with the fluid. The moisture will soon dry up. The drug— if there is a drug—will remain. Then I will rattle the eggs together in an empty drawer, and each day, beginning tomorrow night, I will eat one egg.

I am writing today before I go down to breakfast, partly because I suspect that the hotel does not serve so early. Today I intend to visit the park on the other side of the channel. If it is as dangerous as they say, it is very likely I will not return to make an entry to-

night. If I do return—well, I will plan for that when I am here again.

After I had blown out my candle last night I could not sleep, though I was tired to the bone. Perhaps it was only the excitement of the long walk back from the museum; but I could not free my mind from the image of Ellen. My wandering thoughts associated her with the eggs, and I imagined myself Kreton, sitting up in bed with the cat on my lap. In my daydream (I was not asleep) Ellen brought me my breakfast on a tray, and the breakfast consisted of the six candy eggs.

When my mind had exhausted itself with this kind of imagery, I decided to have the manager procure a girl for me so that I could rid myself of the accumulated tensions of the voyage. After about an hour during which I sat up reading, he arrived with three; and when he had given me a glimpse of them through the half-open door, he slipped inside and shut it behind him, leaving them standing in the corridor. I told him I had only asked for one.

"I know, Mr. Jaffarzadeh, I know. But I thought you might like to have a choice."

None of them—from the glimpse I had had—resembled Ellen; but I thanked him for his thoughtfulness and suggested that he bring them in.

"I wanted to tell you first, sir, that you must allow me to set the price with them—I can get them for much less than you, sir, because they know they cannot deceive me, and they must depend on me to bring them to my guests in

the future." He named a sum that was in fact quite trivial.

"That will be fine," I said. "Bring them in."

He bowed and smiled, making his pinched and miserly face as pleasant as possible and reminding me very much of a picture I had once seen of an imp summoned before the court of Suleiman. "But first, sir, I wished to inform you that if you would like all three—together—you may have them for the price of two. And should you desire only two of the three, you may have them for one and one half the price of one. All are very lovely, and I thought you might want to consider it."

"Very well, I have considered it. Show them in."

"I will light another candle," he said, bustling about the room. "There is no charge, sir, for candles at the rate you're paying. I can put the girls on your bill as well. They'll be down as room service—you understand, I'm sure."

When the second candle was burning and he had positioned it to his liking on the nightstand between the two beds, he opened the door and waved in the girls, saying, "I'll go now. Take what you like and send out the others." (I feel certain this was a stratagem—he felt I would have difficulty in getting any to leave, and so would have to pay for all three.)

Yasmin must never see this—that is decided. It is not just that this entire incident would disturb her greatly, but because of what happened next. I was sitting on the bed nearest the door, hoping to decide quickly which

of the three most resembled the girl who had played Ellen. The first was too short, with a wan, pinched face. The second was tall and blond, but plump. The third, who seemed to stumble as she entered, exactly resembled Yasmin.

For a few seconds I actually believed it was she. Science has so accustomed us to devising and accepting theories to account for the facts we observe, however fantastic, that our minds must begin their manufacture before we are aware of it. Yasmin had grown lonely for me. She had booked passage a few days after my own departure, or perhaps had flown, daring the notorious American landing facilities. Arriving here, she had made inquiries at the consulate, and was approaching my door as the manager lit his candle, and not knowing what was taking place had entered with prostitutes he had engaged.

It was all moonshine, of course. I jumped to my feet and held up the candle, and saw that the third girl, though she had Yasmin's large, dark eyes and rounded little chin, was not she. For all her night-black hair and delicate features, she was indisputably an American; and as she came toward me (encouraged, no doubt, because she had attracted my attention) I saw that like Kreton in the play she had a club foot.

As you see, I returned alive from the park after all. Tonight before I retire I will eat an egg; but first I will briefly set down my experiences.

The park lies on the opposite side of the Washington Channel, between the city and the river. It can be reached by land only at the north end. Not choosing to walk so far and return, I hired a little boat with a tattered red sail to carry me to the southern tip, which is called Hains Point. Here there was a fountain, I am told, in the old times; but nothing remains of it now.

We had clear, sunny spring weather, and made our way over exhilarating swells of wave with nothing of the deadly wallowing that oppressed me so much aboard the *Princess Fatimah*. I sat in the bow and watched the rolling greenery of the park on one side of the channel and the ruins of the old fort on the other, while an elderly man handled the tiller, and his thin, sun-browned granddaughter, aged about eleven, worked the sail.

When we rounded the point, the old man told me that for very little more he would take me across to Arlington to see the remains of what is supposed to be the largest building of the country's antiquity. I refused, determined to save that experience for another time, and we landed where a part of the ancient concrete coping remained intact.

The tracks of old roads run up either shore; but I decided to avoid them, and made my way up the center, keeping to the highest ground in so far as I could. Once, no doubt, the whole area was devoted to pleasure. Very little remains, however, of the pavilions and statuary that must have dotted the ground. There are

little, worn-away hills that may once have been rockeries but are now covered with soil, and many stagnant pools. In a score of places I saw the burrows of the famous giant American rats, though I never saw the animals themselves. To judge from the holes, their size has not been exaggerated—there were several I could have entered with ease.

The wild dogs, against which I had been warned by both the hotel manager and the old boatman, began to follow me after I had walked about a kilometer north. They are short-haired, and typically blotched with black and brown flecked with white. I would say their average weight was about twenty-five kilos. With their erect ears and alert, intelligent faces they did not seem particularly dangerous; but I soon noticed that whichever way I turned, the ones in back of me edged nearer. I sat on a stone with my back to a pool and made several quick sketches of them, then decided to try my pistol. They did not seem to know what it was, so I was able to center the red aiming laser very nicely on one big fellow's chest before I pressed the stud for a high energy pulse.

For a long time afterward, I heard the melancholy howling of these dogs behind me. Perhaps they were mourning their fallen leader. Twice I came across rusting machines that may have been used to take invalids through the gardens in such fair weather as I myself experienced today. Uncle Mirza says I am a good colorist, but I despair of ever matching

the green-haunted blacks with which the declining sun painted the park.

I met no one until I had almost reached the piers of the abandoned railway bridge. Then four or five Americans who pretended to beg surrounded me. The dogs, who as I understand it live mostly upon the refuse cast up by the river, were honest in their intentions and cleaner in their persons. If these people had been like the pitiful creatures I had met in the Silent City, I would have thrown them a few coins; but they were more or less able-bodied men and women who could have worked, and chose instead to rob. I told them that I had been forced to kill a fellow countryman of theirs (not mentioning that he was a dog) who had assaulted me; and asked where I could report the matter to the police. At that they backed off, and permitted me to walk around the northern end of the channel in peace, though not without a thousand savage looks. I returned here without further incident, tired and very well satisfied with my day.

I have eaten one of the eggs! I confess I found it difficult to take the first taste; but marshaling my resolution was like pushing at a wall of glass—all at once the resistance snapped, and I picked the thing up and swallowed it in a few bites. It was piercingly sweet, but there was no other flavor. Now we will see. This is more frightening than the park by far.

* * *

Nothing seemed to be happening, so I went out to dinner. It was twilight, and the carnival spirit of the streets was more marked than ever—colored lights above all the shops, and music from the rooftops where the wealthier natives have private gardens. I have been eating mostly at the hotel, but was told of a "good" American-style restaurant not too far south on Maine Street.

It was just as described—people sitting on padded benches in alcoves. The table tops are of a substance like fine-grained, greasy, artificial stone. They looked very old. I had the Number One Dinner—buff-colored fish soup with the pasty American bread on the side, followed by a sandwich of ground meat and raw vegetables doused with a tomato sauce and served on a soft, oily roll. To tell the truth, I did not much enjoy the meal; but it seems a sort of duty to sample more of the American food than I have thus far.

I am very tempted to end the account of my day here, and in fact I laid down this pen when I had written *thus far*, and made myself ready for bed. Still, what good is a dishonest record? I will let no one see this—just keep it to read over after I get home.

Returning to the hotel from the restaurant, I passed the theater. The thought of seeing Ellen again was irresistible; I bought a ticket and went inside. It was not until I was in my seat that I realized that the bill had changed.

The new play was *Mary Rose*. I saw it done by an English company several years ago, with

great authenticity; and it struck me that (like
Mary herself) it had far outlived its time. The
American production was as inauthentic as the
other had been correct. For that reason, it
retained—or I should have said it had ac-
quired—a good deal of interest.

Americans are superstitious about the interior of their country, not its coasts, so Mary
Rose's island had been shifted to one of the
huge central lakes. The highlander, Cameron,
had accordingly become a Canadian, played by
General Powers' former aide. The Speldings
had become the Morelands, and the Morelands
had become Americans. Kreton was Harry, the
knife-throwing wounded soldier; and my Ellen
had become Mary Rose.

The role suited her so well that I imagined
the play had been selected as a vehicle for her.
Her height emphasized the character's unnatural immaturity, and her slenderness, and the
vulnerability of her pale complexion, would
have told us, I think, if the play had not, that
she had been victimized unaware. More important than any of these things was a wild
and innocent affinity for the supernatural,
which she projected to perfection. It was that
quality alone (as I now understood) that had
made us believe on the preceding night that
Kreton's spaceship might land in the Speldings' rose garden—he would have been drawn
to Ellen, though he had never seen her. Now
it made Mary Rose's disappearances and reap-
pearances plausible and even likely; it was as
likely that unseen spirits lusted for Mary Rose

as that Lieutenant Blake (previously John Randolf) loved her.

Indeed it was more likely. And I had no sooner realized that, than the whole mystery of *Mary Rose*—which had seemed at once inexplicable and banal when I had seen it well played in Teheran—lay clear before me. We of the audience were the envious and greedy spirits. If the Morelands could not see that one wall of their comfortable drawing room was but a sea of dark faces, if Cameron had never noticed that we were the backdrop of his island, the fault was theirs. By rights then, Mary Rose should have been drawn to us when she vanished. At the end of the second act I began to look for her, and in the beginning of the third I found her, standing silent and unobserved behind the last row of seats. I was only four rows from the stage, but I slipped out of my place as unobtrusively as I could, and crept up the aisle toward her.

I was too late. Before I had gone halfway, it was nearly time for her entrance at the end of the scene. I watched the rest of the play from the back of the theater, but she never returned.

Same night. I am having a good deal of trouble sleeping, though while I was on the ship I slept nine hours a night, and was off as soon as my head touched the pillow.

The truth is that while I lay in bed tonight I recalled the old curator's remark that the actresses were all prostitutes. If it is true and not simply an expression of hatred for younger

people whose bodies are still attractive, then I have been a fool to moan over the thought of Mary Rose and Ellen when I might have had the girl herself.

Her name is Ardis Dahl—I just looked it up in the playbill. I am going to the manager's office to consult the city directory there.

Writing before breakfast. Found the manager's office locked last night. It was after two. I put my shoulder against the door and got it open easily enough. (There was no metal socket for the bolt such as we have at home—just a hole mortised in the frame.) The directory listed several Dahls in the city, but since it was nearly eight years out of date it did not inspire a great deal of confidence. I reflected, however, that in a backwater like this people were not likely to move about so much as we do at home, and that if it were not still of some utility, the manager would not be likely to retain it; so I selected the one that appeared from its address to be nearest the theater, and set out.

The streets were completely deserted. I remember thinking that I was now doing what I had previously been so afraid to do, having been frightened of the city by reading. How ridiculous to suppose that robbers would be afoot now, when no one else was. What would they do, stand for hours at the empty corners?

The moon was full and high in the southern sky, showering the street with the lambent white fluid of its light. If it had not been for

the sharp, unclean odor so characteristic of American residential areas, I might have thought myself walking through an illustration from some old book of wonder tales, or an actor in a children's pantomime, so bewitched by the scenery that he has forgotten the audience.

(In writing that—which to tell the truth I did not think of at the time, but only now, as I sat here at my table—I realized that that is in fact what must happen to the American girl I have been in the habit of calling Ellen but must now learn to call Ardis. She could never perform as she does if it were not that in some part of her mind her stage became her reality.)

The shadows about my feet were a century old, tracing faithfully the courses they had determined long before New Tabriz came to jewel the lunar face with its sapphire. Webbed with thoughts of her—my Ellen, my Mary Rose, my Ardis!—and with the magic of that pale light that commands all the tides, I was elevated to a degree I cannot well describe.

Then I was seized by the thought that everything I felt might be no more than the effect of the drug.

At once, like someone who falls from a tower and clutches at the very wisps of air, I tried to return myself to reality. I bit the interiors of my cheeks until the blood filled my mouth, and struck the unfeeling wall of the nearest building with my fist. In a moment the pain sobered me. For a quarter hour or more I stood at the curbside, spitting into the gutter and trying to

clean and bandage my knuckles with strips torn from my handkerchief. A thousand times I thought what a sight I would be if I did in fact succeed in seeing Ellen, and I comforted myself with the thoughts that if she were indeed a prostitute it would not matter to her— I could offer her a few additional rials and all would be well.

Yet that thought was not really much comfort. Even when a woman sells her body, a man flatters himself that she would not do so quite so readily were he not who he is. At the very moment I drooled blood into the street, I was congratulating myself on the strong, square face so many have admired; and wondering how I should apologize if in kissing her I smeared her mouth with red.

Perhaps it was some faint sound that brought me to myself; perhaps it was only the consciousness of being watched. I drew my pistol and turned this way and that, but saw nothing.

Yet the feeling endured. I began to walk again; and if there was any sense of unreality remaining, it was no longer the unearthly exultation I had felt earlier. After a few steps I stopped and listened. A dry sound of rattling and scraping had followed me. It too stopped now.

I was nearing the address I had taken from the directory. I confess my mind was filled with fancies in which I was rescued by Ellen herself, who in the end should be more frightened than I, but who would risk her lovely per-

son to save mine. Yet I knew these *were* but
fancies, and the thing pursuing me was not,
though it crossed my mind more than once
that it might be some *druj* made to seem visible and palpable to me.

Another block, and I had reached the address. It was a house no different from those
on either side—built of the rubble of buildings
that were older still, three-storied, heavy-
doored, and almost without windows. There
was a bookshop on the ground floor (to judge
by an old sign) with living quarters above it. I
crossed the street to see it better, and stood,
wrapped again in my dreams, staring at the
single thread of yellow light that showed between the shutters of a gable window.

As I watched that light, the feeling of being
watched myself grew upon me. Time passed,
slipping through the waist of the universe's
great hourglass like the eroded soil of this
continent slipping down her rivers to the seas.
At last my fear and desire—desire for Ellen,
fear of whatever it was that glared at me with
invisible eyes—drove me to the door of the
house. I hammered the wood with the butt of
my pistol, though I knew how unlikely it was
that any American would answer a knock at
such a time of night, and when I had knocked
several times, I heard slow steps from within.

The door creaked open until it was caught by
a chain. I saw a gray-haired man, fully dressed,
holding an old-fashioned, long-barreled gun. Behind him a woman lifted a stub of smoking candle to let him see; and though she was clearly

much older than Ellen, and was marked, more-
over, by the deformities so prevalent here, there
was a certain nobility in her features and a certain beauty as well, so that I was reminded of
the fallen statue that is said to have stood on an
island farther north, and which I have seen pic-
tured.

I told the man that I was a traveler—true
enough!—and that I had just arrived by boat
from Arlington and had no place to stay, and
so had walked into the city until I had noticed
the light of his window. I would pay, I said, a
silver rial if they would only give me a bed for
the night and breakfast in the morning, and I
showed them the coin. My plan was to become
a guest in the house so that I might discover
whether Ellen was indeed one of the inhabitants; if she were, it would have been an easy
matter to prolong my stay.

The woman tried to whisper in her husband's ear, but save for a look of nervous irritation he ignored her. "I don't dare let a
stranger in." From his voice I might have been
a lion, and his gun a trainer's chair. "Not with
no one here but my wife and myself."

"I see," I told him. "I quite understand your
position."

"You might try the house on the corner," he
said, shutting the door, "but don't tell them
Dahl sent you." I heard the heavy bar dropped
into place at the final word.

I turned away—and then by the mercy of Allah who is indeed compassionate happened to
glance back one last time at the thread of yel-

low between the shutters of that high window. A flicker of scarlet higher still caught my attention, perhaps only because the light of the setting moon now bathed the rooftop from a new angle. I think the creature I glimpsed there had been waiting to leap upon me from behind, but when our eyes met it launched itself toward me. I had barely time to lift my pistol before it struck me and slammed me to the broken pavement of the street.

For a brief period I think I lost consciousness. If my shot had not killed the thing as it fell, I would not be sitting here writing this journal this morning. After half a minute or so I came to myself enough to thrust its weight away, stand up, and rub my bruises. No one had come to my aid; but neither had anyone rushed from the surrounding houses to kill and rob me. I was as alone with the creature that lay dead at my feet as I had been when I only stood watching the window in the house from which it had sprung.

After I found my pistol and assured myself that it was still in working order, I dragged the thing to a spot of moonlight. When I glimpsed it on the roof, it had seemed a feral dog, like the one I had shot in the park. When it lay dead before me, I had thought it a human being. In the moonlight I saw it was neither, or perhaps both. There was a blunt muzzle; and the height of the skull above the eyes, which anthropologists say is the surest badge of humanity and speech, had been stunted until it was not greater than I have

seen in a macaque. Yet the arms and shoulders and pelvis—even a few filthy rags of clothing—all bespoke mankind. It was a female, with small, flattened breasts still apparent on either side of the burn channel.

At least ten years ago I read about such things in Osman Aga's *Mystery Beyond the Sun's Setting;* but it was very different to stand shivering on a deserted street corner of the old capital and examine the thing in the flesh. By Osman Aga's account (which no one, I think, but a few old women has ever believed) these creatures were in truth human beings—or at least the descendants of human beings. In the last century, when the famine gripped their country and the irreversible damage done to the chromosomal structures of the people had already become apparent, some few turned to the eating of human flesh. No doubt the corpses of the famine supplied their food at first; and no doubt those who ate of them congratulated themselves that by doing so they had escaped the effects of the enzymes that were then still used to bring slaughter animals to maturity in a matter of months. What they failed to realize was that the bodies of the human beings they ate had accumulated far more of these unnatural substances than were ever found in the flesh of the short-lived cattle. From them, according to *Mystery Beyond the Sun's Setting,* rose such creatures as the thing I had killed.

But Osman Aga has never been believed. So far as I know, he is a mere popular writer,

with a reputation for glorifying Caspian resorts in recompense for free lodging, and for indulging in absurd expeditions to breed more books and publicize the ones he has already written—crossing the desert on a camel and the Alps on an elephant—and no one else has ever, to my knowledge, reported such things from this continent. The ruined cities filled with rats and rabid bats, and the terrible whirling dust storms of the interior, have been enough for other travel writers. Now I am sorry I did not contrive a way to cut off the thing's head; I feel sure its skull would have been of interest to science.

As soon as I had written the preceding paragraph, I realized that there might still be a chance to do what I had failed to do last night. I went to the kitchen, and for a small bribe was able to secure a large, sharp knife, which I concealed beneath my jacket.

It was still early as I ran down the street, and for a minutes I had high hopes that the thing's body might still be lying where I had left it; but my efforts were all for nothing. It was gone, and there was no sign of its presence—no blood, no scar from my beam on the house. I poked into alleys and waste cans. Nothing. At last I came back to the hotel for breakfast, and I have now (it is mid-morning) returned to my room to make my plans for the day.

Very well. I failed to meet Ellen last night— I shall not fail today. I am going to buy an-

other ticket for the play, and tonight I will not take my seat, but wait behind the last row where I saw her standing. If she comes to watch at the end of the second act as she did last night, I will be there to compliment her on her performance and present her with some gift. If she does not come, I will make my way backstage—from what I have seen of these Americans, a quarter rial should get me anywhere, but I am willing to loosen a few teeth if I must.

What absurd creatures we are! I have just reread what I wrote this morning, and I might as well have been writing of the philosophic speculations of the Congress of Birds or the affairs of the demons in Domdaniel, or any other subject on which neither I nor anyone else knows or can know a thing. O Book, you have heard what I supposed would occur, now let me tell you what actually took place.

I set out as I had planned to procure a gift for Ellen. On the advice of the hotel manager, I followed Maine Street north until I reached the wide avenue that passes close by the obelisk. Around the base of this still imposing monument is held a perpetual fair in which the merchants use the stone blocks fallen from the upper part of the structure as tables. What remains of the shaft is still, I should say, upwards of one hundred meters high; but it is said to have formerly stood three or four times that height. Much of the fallen material has been carted away to build private homes.

There seems to be no logic to the prices in this country, save for the general rule that foodstuffs are cheap and imported machinery—cameras and the like—costly. Textiles are expensive, which no doubt explains why so many of the people wear ragged clothes that they mend and dye in an effort to make them look new. Certain kinds of jewelry are quite reasonable; others sell for much higher prices than they would in Teheran. Rings of silver or white gold set, usually, with a single modest diamond, may be had in great numbers for such low prices that I was tempted into buying a few to take home as an investment. Yet I saw bracelets that would have sold at home for no more than half a rial, for which the seller asked ten times that much. There were many interesting antiques, all of which are alleged to have been dug from the ruined cities of the interior at the cost of someone's life. When I had talked to five or six vendors of such items, I was able to believe that I knew how the country was depopulated.

After a good deal of this pleasant, wordy shopping, during which I spent very little, I selected a bracelet made of old coins—many of them silver—as my gift to Ellen. I reasoned that women always like jewelry, and that such a showy piece might be of service to an actress in playing some part or other, and that the coins must have a good deal of intrinsic value. Whether she will like it or not—if she ever receives it—I do not know; it is still in the pocket of my jacket.

When the shadow of the obelisk had grown long, I returned here to the hotel and had a good dinner of lamb and rice, and retired to groom myself for the evening. The five remaining candy eggs stood staring at me from the top of my dresser. I remembered my resolve, and took one. Quite suddenly I was struck by the conviction that the demon I believed I had killed the night before had been no more than a phantom engendered by the action of the drug.

What if I had been firing my pistol at mere empty air? That seemed a terrible thought—indeed it seems so to me still. A worse one is that the drug really may have rendered visible—as some say those ancient preparations were intended to—a real but spiritual being. If such things in fact walk what we take to be unoccupied rooms and rooftops, and the empty streets of night, it would explain many sudden deaths and diseases, and perhaps the sudden changes for the worse we sometimes see in others and others in us, and even the birth of evil men. This morning I called the thing a *druj;* it may be true.

Yet if the drug had been in the egg I ate last night, then the egg I held was harmless. Concentrating on that thought, I forced myself to eat it all, then stretched myself upon the bed to wait.

Very briefly I slept and dreamed. Ellen was bending over me, caressing me with a soft, long-fingered hand. It was only for an instant,

but sufficient to make me hope that dreams are prophecies.

If the drug was in the egg I consumed, that dream was its only result. I got up and washed, and changed my clothes, sprinkling my fresh shirt liberally with our Pamir rosewater, which I have observed the Americans hold in high regard. Making certain my ticket and pistol were both in place, I left for the theater.

The play was still *Mary Rose*. I intentionally entered late (after Harry and Mrs. Otery had been talking for several minutes), then lingered at the back of the last row as though I were too polite to disturb the audience by taking my seat. Mrs. Otery made her exit; Harry pulled his knife from the wood of the packing case and threw it again, and when the mists of the past had marched across the stage, Harry was gone, and Moreland and the parson were chatting to the tune of Mrs. Moreland's knitting needles. Mary Rose would be on stage soon. My hope that she would come out to watch the opening scene had come to nothing; I would have to wait until she vanished at the end of Act II before I could expect to see her.

I was looking for a vacant seat when I become conscious of someone standing near me. In the dim light I could tell little except that he was rather slender, and a few centimeters shorter than I.

Finding no seat, I moved back a step or two. The newcomer touched my arm and asked in a whisper if I could light his cigarette. I had already seen that it was customary to smoke

in the theaters here, and I had fallen into the habit of carrying matches to light the candles in my room. The flare of the flame showed the narrow eyes and high cheekbones of Harry—or as I preferred to think of him, Kreton. Taken somewhat aback, I murmured some inane remark about the excellence of his performance.

"Did you like it? It is the best of all parts—I pull the curtain to open the show, then pull it again to tell everyone it's time to go home."

Several people in the audience were looking angrily at us, so we retreated to a point at the head of the aisle that was at least legally in the lobby, where I told him I had seen him in *Visit to a Small Planet* as well.

"Now *there* is a play. The character—as I am sure you saw—is good and bad at once. He is benign, he is mischievous, he is hellish."

"You carried it off wonderfully well, I thought."

"Thank you. This turkey here—do you know how many roles it has?"

"Well, there's yourself, Mrs. Otery, Mr. Amy—"

"No, no." He touched my arm to stop me. "I mean *roles*, parts that require real acting. There's one—the girl. She gets to skip about the stage as an eighteen-year-old whose brain atrophied at ten; and at least half what she does is wasted on the audience because they don't realize what's wrong with her until Act I is almost over."

"She's wonderful," I said. "I mean Mademoiselle Dahl."

Kreton nodded and drew on his cigarette. "She is a very competent ingenue, though it would be better if she weren't quite so tall."

"Do you think there's any chance that she might come out here—as you did?"

"Ah," he said, and looked me up and down. For a moment I could have sworn that the telepathic ability he was credited with in *Visit to a Small Planet* was no fiction; nevertheless, I repeated my question: "Is it probable or not?"

"There's no reason to get angry—no, it's not likely. Is that enough payment for your match?"

"She vanishes at the end of the second act, and doesn't come on stage again until near the close of the third."

Kreton smiled. "You've read the play?"

"I was here last night. She must be off for nearly forty minutes, including the intermission."

"That's right. But she won't be here. It's true she goes out front sometimes—as I did myself tonight—but I happen to know she has company backstage."

"Might I ask who?"

"You might. It's even possible I might answer. You're Moslem, I suppose—do you drink?"

"I'm not a *strict* Moslem; but no, I don't. I'll buy you a drink gladly though, if you want one, and have coffee with you while you drink it."

We left by a side door and elbowed our way through the crowd in the street. A flight of narrow and dirty steps descending from the sidewalk led us to a cellar tavern that had all the atmosphere of a private club. There was a bar with a picture (now much dimmed by dirt and smoke) of the cast of a play I did not recognize behind it, three tables, and a few alcoves. Kreton and I slipped into one of these and ordered from a barman with a misshapen head. I suppose I must have stared at him, because Kreton said, "I sprained my ankle stepping out of a saucer, and now I am a convalescent soldier. Should we make up something for him too? Can't we just say the potter is angry sometimes?"

"The potter?" I asked.

" 'None answered this; but after Silence spake/A Vessel of a more ungainly Make:/They sneer at me for leaning all awry;/What! Did the Hand then of the Potter shake?' "

I shook my head. "I've never heard that; but you're right, he looks as though his head had been shaped in clay, then knocked in on one side while it was still wet."

"This is a republic of hideousness, as you have no doubt already seen. Our national symbol is supposed to be an extinct eagle; it is in fact the nightmare."

"I find it a very beautiful country," I said. "Though I confess that many of your people are unsightly. Still, there are the ruins, and you have such skies as we never see at home."

"Our chimneys have been filled with wind for a long time."

"That may be for the best. Blue skies are better than most of the things made in factories."

"And not all our people are unsightly," Kreton murmured.

"Oh no. Mademoiselle Dahl—"

"I had myself in mind."

I saw that he was baiting me, but I said, "No, you aren't hideous—in fact, I would call you handsome in an exotic way. Unfortunately, my tastes run more toward Mademoiselle Dahl."

"Call her Ardis—she won't mind."

The barman brought Kreton a glass of green liqueur, and me a cup of the weak, bitter American coffee.

"You were going to tell me who she is entertaining."

"Behind the scenes." Kreton smiled. "I just thought of that—I've used the phrase a thousand times, as I suppose everyone has. This time it happens to be literally correct, and its birth is suddenly made plain, like Oedipus's. No, I don't think I promised I would tell you that—though I suppose I said I might. Aren't there other things you would really rather know? The secret hidden beneath Mount Rushmore, or how you might meet her yourself?"

"I will give you twenty rials to introduce me to her, with some assurance that something will come of the introduction. No one need ever find out."

Kreton laughed. "Believe me, I would be more likely to boast of my profit than keep it secret—though I would probably have to divide my fee with the lady to fulfill the guarantee."

"You'll do it then?"

He shook his head, still laughing. "I only pretend to be corrupt; it goes with this face. Come backstage after the show tonight, and I'll see that you meet Ardis. You're very wealthy, I presume, and if you're not, we'll say you are anyway. What are you doing here?"

"Studying your art and architecture."

"Great reputation in your own country, no doubt?"

"I am a pupil of Akhon Mirza Ahmak; he has a great reputation, surely. He even came here, thirty years ago, to examine the miniatures in your National Gallery of Art."

"Pupil of Akhon Mirza Ahmak, pupil of Akhon Mirza Ahmak," Kreton muttered to himself. "That is very good—I must remember it. But now"—he glanced at the old clock behind the bar—"it's time we got back. I'll have to freshen my makeup before I go on in the last act. Would you prefer to wait in the theater, or just come around to the stage door when the play's over? I'll give you a card that will get you in."

"I'll wait in the theater," I said, feeling that would offer less chance for mishap; also because I wanted to see Ellen play the ghost again.

"Come along then—I have a key for that side door."

I rose to go with him, and he threw an arm about my shoulder that I felt it would be impolite to thrust away. I could feel his hand, as cold as a dead man's, through my clothing, and was reminded unpleasantly of the twisted hands of the beggar in the Silent City.

We were going up the narrow stairs when I felt a gentle touch inside my jacket. My first thought was that he had seen the outline of my pistol, and meant to take it and shoot me. I gripped his wrist and shouted something—I do not remember what. Bound together and struggling, we staggered up the steps and into the street.

In a few seconds we were the center of a mob—some taking his side, some mine, most only urging us to fight, or asking each other what the disturbance was. My pocket sketchpad, which he must have thought held money, fell to the ground between us. Just then the American police arrived—not by air as the police would have come at home, but astride shaggy, hulking horses, and swinging whips. The crowd scattered at the first crackling arc from the lashes, and in a few seconds they had beaten Kreton to the ground. Even at the time I could not help thinking what a terrible thing it must be to be one of these people, whose police are so quick to prefer any prosperous-looking foreigner to one of their own citizens.

They asked me what had happened (my questioner even dismounted to show his re-

spect for me, and I explained that Kreton had tried to rob me, but that I did not want him punished. The truth was that seeing him sprawled unconscious with a burn across his face had put an end to any resentment I might have felt toward him; out of pity, I would gladly have given him the few rials I carried. They told me that if he had attempted to rob me he must be charged, and that if I would not accuse him they would do so themselves.

I then said that Kreton was a friend; and that on reflection I felt certain that what he had attempted had been intended as a prank. (In maintaining this I was considerably handicapped by not knowing his real name, which I had read on the playbill but forgotten, so that I was forced to refer to him as "this poor man.")

At last the policeman said, "We can't leave him in the street, so we'll have to bring him in. How will it look if there's no complaint?"

Then I understood that they were afraid of what their superiors might say if it became known that they had beaten him unconscious when no charge was made against him; and when I became aware that if I would not press charges, the charges they would bring themselves would be far more serious—assault or attempted murder—I agreed to do what they wished, and signed a form alleging the theft of my sketchbook.

When they had gone at last, carrying the unfortunate Kreton across a saddlebow, I tried to reenter the theater. The side door through

which we had left was locked, and though I would gladly have paid the price of another ticket, the box office was closed. Seeing that there was nothing further to be done, I returned here, telling myself that my introduction to Ellen, if it ever came, would have to wait for another day.

Very truly it is written that we walk by paths that are always turning. In recording these several pages I have managed to restrain my enthusiasm, though when I described my waiting at the back of the theater for Ardis, and again when I recounted how Kreton had promised to introduce me to her, I was forced for minutes at a time to lay down my pen and walk about the room singing and whistling, and—to reveal everything—jumping over the beds! But now I can conceal no longer. I have seen her! I have touched her hand; I am to see her again tomorrow; and there is every hope that she will become my mistress!

I had undressed and laid myself on the bed (thinking to bring this journal up to date in the morning) and had even fallen into the first doze of sleep, when there was a knock at the door. I slipped into my robe and pressed the release.

It was the only time in my life that for even an instant I thought I might be dreaming—actually asleep—when in truth I was up and awake.

How feeble it is to write that she is more beautiful in person than she appears on the stage. It is true, and yet it is a supreme irrelevance. I have seen more beautiful women—

indeed Yasmin is, I suppose, by the formal standards of art, more lovely. It is not Ardis' beauty that draws me to her—the hair like gold, the translucent skin that then still showed traces of the bluish makeup she had worn as a ghost, the flashing eyes like the clear, clean skies of America. It is something deeper than that; something that would remain if all that were somehow taken away. No doubt she has habits that would disgust me in someone else, and the vanity that is said to be so common in her profession, and yet I would do anything to possess her.

Enough of this. What is it but empty boasting, now that I am on the point of winning her?

She stood in my doorway. I have been trying to think how I can express what I felt then. It was as though some tall flower, a lily perhaps, had left the garden and come to tap at my door, a thing that had never happened before in all the history of the world, and would never happen again.

"You are Nadan Jaffarzadeh?"

I admitted that I was, and shamefacedly, twenty seconds too late, moved out of her way.

She entered, but instead of taking the chair I indicated, turned to face me; her blue eyes seemed as large as the colored eggs on the dresser, and they were filled with a melting hope. "You are the man, then, that Bobby O'Keene tried to rob tonight."

I nodded.

"I know you—I mean, I know your face. This is insane. You came to *Visit* on the last night

and brought your father, and then to *Mary Rose* on the first night, and sat in the third or fourth row. I thought you were an American, and when the police told me your name I imagined some greasy fat man with gestures. Why on earth would Bobby want to steal from *you?*"

"Perhaps he needed the money."

She threw back her head and laughed. I had heard her laugh in *Mary Rose* when Simon was asking her father for her hand; but that had held a note of childishness that (however well suited to the part) detracted from its beauty. This laugh was the merriment of houris sliding down a rainbow. "I'm sure he did. He always needs money. You're sure, though, that he meant to rob you? You couldn't have . . . "

She saw my expression and let the question trail away. The truth is that I was disappointed that I could not oblige her, and at last I said, "If you want me to be mistaken, Ardis, then I was mistaken. He only bumped against me on the steps, perhaps, and tried to catch my sketchbook when it fell."

She smiled, and her face was the sun smiling upon roses. "You would say that for me? And you know my name?"

"From the program. I came to the theater to see you—and that was not my father, who it grieves me to say is long dead, but only an old man, an American, whom I had met that day."

"You brought him sandwiches at the first intermission—I was watching you through the

peephole in the curtain. You must be a very thoughtful person."

"Do you watch everyone in the audience so carefully?"

She blushed at that, and for a moment could not meet my eyes.

"But you will forgive Bobby, and tell the police that you want them to let him go? You must love the theater, Mr. Jef—Jaff—"

"You've forgotten my name already. It is Jaffarzadeh, a very commonplace name in my country."

"I hadn't forgotten it—only how to pronounce it. You see, when I came here I had learned it without knowing who you were, and so I had no trouble with it. Now you're a real person to me and I can't say it as an actress should." She seemed to notice the chair behind her for the first time, and sat down.

I sat opposite her. "I'm afraid I know very little about the theater."

"We are trying to keep it alive here, Mr. Jaffar, and—"

"Jaffarzadeh. Call me Nadan—then you won't have so many syllables to trip over."

She took my hand in hers, and I knew quite well that the gesture was as studied as a salaam and that she felt she was playing me like a fish; but I was beside myself with delight. To be played by *her!* To have *her* eager to cultivate my affection! And the fish will pull her in yet—wait and see!

"I will," she said, "Nadan. And though you may know little of the theater, you feel as I

do—as we do—or you would not come. It has been such a long struggle; all the history of the stage is a struggle, the gasping of a beautiful child born at the point of death. The moralists, censorship and oppression, technology, and now poverty have all tried to destroy her. Only we, the actors and audiences, have kept her alive. We have been doing well here in Washington, Nadan."

"Very well indeed," I said. "Both the productions I have seen have been excellent."

"But only for the past two seasons. When I joined the company it had nearly fallen apart. We revived it—Bobby and Paul and I. We could do it because we cared, and because we were able to find a few naturally talented people who can take direction. Bobby is the best of us—he can walk away with any part that calls for a touch of the sinister . . ."

She seemed to run out of breath. I said, "I don't think there will be any trouble about getting him free."

"Thank God. We're getting the theater on its feet again now. We're attracting new people, and we've built up a following—people who come to see every production. There's even some money ahead at last. But *Mary Rose* is supposed to run another two weeks, and after that we're doing *Faust*, with Bobby as Mephistopheles. We've simply no one who can take his place, no one who can come close to him."

"I'm sure the police will release him if I ask them to."

"They *must*. We have to have him tomorrow

night. Bill—someone you don't know—tried to go on for him in the third act tonight. It was just ghastly. In Iran you're very polite; that's what I've heard."

"We enjoy thinking so."

"We're not. We never were; and as . . ."

Her voice trailed away, but a wave of one slender arm evoked everything—the cracked plaster walls became as air, and the decayed city, the ruined continent, entered the room with us. "I understand," I said.

"They—we—were betrayed. In our souls we have never been sure by whom. When we feel cheated we are ready to kill; and maybe we feel cheated all the time."

She slumped in her chair, and I realized, as I should have long before, how exhausted she was. She had given a performance that had ended in disaster, then had been forced to plead with the police for my name and address, and at last had come here from the station house, very probably on foot. I asked when I could obtain O'Keene's release.

"We can go tomorrow morning, if you'll do it."

"You wish to come too?"

She nodded, smoothed her skirt, and stood. "I'll have to know. I'll come for you about nine, if that's all right."

"If you'll wait outside for me to dress, I'll take you home."

"That's not necessary."

"It will only take a moment," I said.

The blue eyes held something pleading

again. "You're going to come in with me— that's what you're thinking, I know. You have two beds here—bigger, cleaner beds than the one I have in my little apartment; if I were to ask you to push them together, would you still take me home afterward?"

It was as though I were dreaming indeed—a dream in which everything I wanted—the cosmos purified—delivered itself to me. I said, "You won't have to leave at all—you can spend the night with me. Then we can breakfast together before we go to release your friend."

She laughed again, lifting that exquisite head. "There are a hundred things at home I need. Do you think I'd have breakfast with you without my cosmetics, and in these dirty clothes?"

"Then I will take you home—yes, though you lived in Kazvin. Or on Mount Kaf."

She smiled. "Get dressed, then. I'll wait outside, and I'll show you my apartment; perhaps you won't want to come back here afterward."

She went out, her wooden-soled American shoes clicking on the bare floor, and I threw on trousers, shirt, and jacket, and jammed my feet into my boots. When I opened the door, she was gone. I rushed to the barred window at the end of the corridor, and was in time to see her disappear down a side street. A last swirl of her skirt in a gush of night wind, and she had vanished into the velvet dark.

For a long time I stood there looking out over the ruinous buildings. I was not angry— I do not think I could be angry with her. I was,

though here it is hard to tell the truth, in some way glad. Not because I feared the embrace of love—I have no doubt of my ability to suffice any woman who can be sated by man—but because an easy exchange of my cooperation for her person would have failed to satisfy my need for romance, for adventure of a certain type, in which danger and love are twined like coupling serpents. Ardis, my Ellen, will provide that, surely, as neither Yasmin nor the pitiful wanton who was her double could. I sense that the world is opening for me only now; that I am being born; that that corridor was the birth canal, and that Ardis in leaving me was drawing me out toward her.

When I returned to my own door, I noticed a bit of paper on the floor before it. I transcribe it exactly here, though I cannot transmit its scent of lilacs.

> *You are a most attractive man and I want very much to stretch the truth and tell you you can have me freely when Bobby is free but I won't sell myself etc. Really I will sell myself for Bobby but I have other fish to fry tonight. I'll see you in the morning and if you can get Bobby out or even try hard you'll have (real) love from the vanishing*
>
> *Mary Rose*

Morning. Woke early and ate here at the hotel as usual, finishing about eight. Writing this journal will give me something to do while I

wait for Ardis. Had an American breakfast today, the first time I have risked one. Flakes of
pastry dough toasted crisp and drenched with
cream, and with it strudel and the usual American coffee. Most natives have spiced pork in
one form or another, which I cannot bring myself to try; but several of the people around
me were having egg dishes and oven-warmed
bread, which I will sample tomorrow.

I had a very unpleasant dream last night; I
have been trying to put it out of my mind ever
since I woke. It was dark, and I was under an
open sky with Ardis, walking over ground
much rougher than anything I saw in the park
on the farther side of the channel. One of the
hideous creatures I shot night before last was
pursuing us—or rather, lurking about us, for
it appeared first to the left of us, then to the
right, silhouetted against the night sky. Each
time we saw it, Ardis grasped my arm and
urged me to shoot, but the little indicator light
on my pistol was glowing red to show that
there was not enough charge left for a shot.
All very silly, of course, but I am going to buy
a fresh powerpack as soon as I have the opportunity.

It is late afternoon—after six—but we have
not had dinner yet. I am just out of the tub,
and sit here naked, with today's candy egg laid
(pinker even than I) beside this book on my
table. Ardis and I had a sorry, weary time of
it, and I have come back here to make myself
presentable. At seven we will meet for dinner;

the curtain goes up at eight, so it can't be a
long one, but I am going backstage to watch
the play from the wings, where I will be able
to talk to her when she isn't performing.

I just took a bite of the egg—no unusual
taste, nothing but an unpleasant sweetness.
The more I reflect on it, the more inclined I
am to believe that the drug was in the first I
ate. No doubt the monster I saw had been
lurking in my brain since I read *Mysteries*, and
the drug freed it. True, there were bloodstains
on my clothes (the Peri's asphodel!) but they
could as easily have come from my cheek,
which is still sore. I have had my experience,
and all I have left is my candy. I am almost
tempted to throw out the rest. Another bite.

Still twenty minutes before I must dress and
go for Ardis—she showed me where she lives,
only a few doors from the theater. To work
then.

Ardis was a trifle late this morning, but came
as she had promised. I asked where we were
to go to free Kreton, and when she told me—
a still-living building at the eastern end of the
Silent City—I hired one of the rickety American caleches to drive us there. Like most of
them, it was drawn by a starved horse; but we
made good time.

The American police are organized on a peculiar system. The national secret police (offi-
cially, the Federated Enquiry Divisions) are in
a tutorial position to all the others, having
power to review their decisions, promote, de-
mote, and discipline, and as the ultimate re-

ward, enroll personnel from the other organizations. In addition they maintain a uniformed force of their own. Thus when an American has been arrested by uniformed police, his friends can seldom learn whether he has been taken by the local police, by the F.E.D. uniformed national force, or by members of the F.E.D. secret police posing as either of the foregoing.

Since I had known nothing of these distinctions previously, I had no way of guessing which of the three had O'Keene; but the local police to whom Ardis had spoken the night before had given her to understand that he had been taken by them. She explained all this to me as we rattled along, then added that we were now going to the F.E.D. building to secure his release. I must have looked as confused as I felt at this, because she added, "Part of it is a station for the Washington Police Department—they rent the space from the F.E.D."

My own impression (when we arrived) was that they did no such thing—that the entire apparatus was no more real than one of the scenes in Ardis's theater, and that all the men and women to whom we spoke were in fact agents of the secret police, wielding ten times the authority they pretended to possess, and going through a solemn ritual of deception. As Ardis and I moved from office to office, explaining our simple errand, I came to think that she felt as I did, and that she had refrained from expressing these feelings to me

in the cab not only because of the danger, the fear that I might betray her or the driver be a spy, but because she was ashamed of her nation, and eager to make it appear to me, a foreigner, that her government was less devious and meretricious than is actually the case.

If this is so—and in that windowless warren of stone I was certain it was—then the very explanation she proffered in the cab (which I have given in its proper place) differentiating clearly between local police, uniformed F.E.D. police, and secret police, was no more than a children's fable, concealing an actuality less forthright and more convoluted.

Our questioners were courteous to me, much less so to Ardis, and (so it seemed to me) obsessed by the idea that something more lay behind the simple incident we described over and over again—so much so in fact that I came to believe it myself. I have neither time nor patience enough to describe all these interviews, but I will attempt to give a sample of one.

We went into a small, windowless office crowded between two others that appeared empty. A middle-aged American woman was seated behind a metal desk. She appeared normal and reasonably attractive until she spoke; then her scarred gums showed that she had once had two or three times the proper number of teeth—forty or fifty, I suppose, in each jaw—and that the dental surgeon who had extracted the supernumerary ones had not always, perhaps, selected those he suffered to remain as wisely as he might. She asked, "How

is it outside? The weather? You see, I don't know, sitting in here all day."

Ardis said, "Very nice."

"Do you like it, *Hajji?* Have you had a pleasant stay in our great country?"

"I don't think it has rained since I've been here."

She seemed to take the remark as a covert accusation. "You came too late for the rains, I'm afraid. This is a very fertile area, however. Some of our oldest coins show heads of wheat. Have you seen them?" She pushed a small copper coin across the desk, and I pretended to examine it. There are one or two like it in the bracelet I bought for Ardis, and which I still have not presented to her. "I must apologize on behalf of the District for what happened to you," the woman continued. "We are making every effort to control crime. You have not been victimized before this?"

I shook my head, half suffocated in that airless office, and said I had not been.

"And now you are here." She shuffled the papers she held, then pretended to read from one of them. "You are here to secure the release of the thief who assaulted you. A very commendable act of magnanimity. May I ask why you brought this young woman with you? She does not seem to be mentioned in any of these reports."

I explained that Ardis was a coworker of O'Keene's, and that she had interceded for him.

"Then it is you, Ms. Dahl, who are really in-

terested in securing this prisoner's release. Are you related to him?"

And so on.

At the conclusion of each interview we were told either that the matter was completely out of the hands of the person to whom we had just spent half an hour or an hour talking, that it was necessary to obtain a clearance from someone else, or that an additional deposition had to be made. About two o'clock we were sent to the other side of the river—into what my guide-books insist is an entirely different jurisdiction—to visit a penal facility. There we were forced to look for Kreton among five hundred or so miserable prisoners, all of whom stank and had lice. Not finding him, we returned to the F.E.D. building past the half-overturned and yet still brooding figure called the Seated Man, and the ruins and beggars of the Silent City, for another round of interrogations. By five, when we were told to leave, we were both exhausted, though Ardis seemed surprisingly hopeful. When I left her at the door of her building a few minutes ago, I asked her what they would do tonight without Kreton.

"Without Harry, you mean." She smiled. "The best we can, I suppose, if we must. At least Paul will have someone ready to stand in for him tonight."

We shall see how well it goes.

I have picked up this pen and replaced it on the table ten times at least. It seems very likely

that I should destroy this journal instead of continuing with it, were I wise; but I have discovered a hiding place for it which I think will be secure.

When I came back from Ardis's apartment tonight there were only two candy eggs remaining. I am certain—absolutely certain—that three were left when I went to meet Ardis. I am almost equally sure that after I had finished making the entry in this book, I put it, as I always do, at the left side of the drawer. It was on the right side.

It is possible that all this is merely the doing of the maid who cleans the room. She might easily have supposed that a single candy egg would not be missed, and have shifted this book while cleaning the drawer, or peeped inside out of curiosity.

I will assume the worst, however. An agent sent to investigate my room might be equipped to photograph these pages—but he might not, and it is not likely that he himself would have a reading knowledge of Farsi. Now I have gone through the book and eliminated all the passages relating to my reason for visiting this leprous country. Before I leave this room tomorrow I will arrange indicators—hairs and other objects whose positions I shall carefully record—that will tell me if the room has been searched again.

Now I may as well set down the events of the evening, which were truly extraordinary enough.

I met Ardis as we had planned, and she di-

rected me to a small restaurant not far from her apartment. We had no sooner seated ourselves than two heavy-looking men entered. At no time could I see plainly the face of either, but it appeared to me that one was the American I had met aboard the *Princess Fatimah* and that the other was the grain dealer I had so assiduously avoided there, Golam Gassem. It is impossible, I think, for my divine Ardis ever to look less than beautiful; but she came as near to it then as the laws permit—the blood drained from her face, her mouth opened slightly, and for a moment she appeared to be a lovely corpse. I began to ask what the trouble was, but before I could utter a word she touched my lips to silence me, and then, having somewhat regained her composure, said, "They have not seen us. I am leaving now. Follow me as though we were finished eating." She stood, feigned to pat her lips with a napkin (so that the lower half of her face was hidden) and walked out into the street.

I followed her, and found her laughing not three doors away from the entrance to the restaurant. The change in her could not have been more startling if she had been released from an enchantment. "It is so funny," she said. "Though it wasn't then. Come on, we'd better go; you can feed me after the show."

I asked her what those men were to her.

"Friends," she said, still laughing.

"If they are friends, why were you so anxious that they not see you? Were you afraid they would make us late?" I know that such a

trivial explanation could not be true, but I wanted to leave her a means of evading the question if she did not want to confide in me.

She shook her head. "No, no. I didn't want either to think I did not trust him. I'll tell you more later, if you want to involve yourself in our little charade."

"With all my heart."

She smiled at that—that sun-drenched smile for which I would gladly have entered a lion pit. In a few more steps we were at the rear entrance to the theater, and there was no time to say more. She opened the door, and I heard Kreton arguing with a woman I later learned was the wardrobe mistress. "You are free," I said, and he turned to look at me.

"Yes. Thanks to you, I think. And I do thank you."

Ardis gazed on him as though he were a child saved from drowning. "Poor Bobby. Was it very bad?"

"It was frightening, that's all. I was afraid I'd never get out. Do you know Terry is gone?"

She shook her head, and said, "What do you mean?" but I was certain—and here I am not exaggerating or coloring the facts, though I confess I have occasionally done so elsewhere in this chronicle—that she had known it before he spoke.

"He simply isn't here. Paul is running around like a lunatic. I hear you missed me last night."

"God, yes," Ardis said, and darted off too swiftly for me to follow.

Kreton took my arm. I expected him to apologize for having tried to rob me, but he said, "You've met her, I see."

"She persuaded me to drop the charges against you."

"Whatever it was you offered me—twenty rials? I'm morally entitled to it, but I won't claim it. Come and see me when you're ready for something more wholesome—and meanwhile, how do you like her?"

"That is something for me to tell her," I said, "not you."

Ardis returned as I spoke, bringing with her a balding black man with a mustache. "Paul, this is Nadan. His English is very good—not so British as most of them. He'll do, don't you think?"

"He'll have to—you're sure he'll do it?"

"He'll love it," Ardis said positively, and disappeared again.

It seemed that Terry was the actor who played Mary Rose's husband and lover, Simon; and I—who had never acted in so much as a school play—was to be pressed into the part. It was about half an hour before curtain time, so I had all of fifty minutes to learn my lines before my entrance at the end of the first act.

Paul, the director, warned me that if my name were used, the audience would be hostile; and since the character (in the version of the play they were presenting) was supposed to be an American, they would see errors where none existed. A moment later, while I

was still in frantic rehearsal, I heard him saying, "The part of Simon Blake will be taken by Ned Jefferson."

The act of stepping onto the stage for the first time was really the worst part of the entire affair. Fortunately I had the advantage of playing a nervous young man come to ask for the hand of his sweetheart, so that my shaky laughter and stammer became "acting."

My second scene—with Mary Rose and Cameron on the magic island—ought by rights to have been much more difficult than the first. I had had only the intermission in which to study my lines, and the scene called for pessimistic apprehension rather than mere anxiety. But all the speeches were short, and Paul had been able by that time to get them lettered on large sheets of paper, which he and the stage manager held up in the wings. Several times I was forced to extemporize, but though I forgot the playwright's words, I never lost my sense of the *trend* of the play, and was always able to contrive something to which Ardis and Cameron could adapt their replies.

In comparison to the first and second acts, my brief appearance in the third was a holiday; yet I have seldom been so exhausted as I was tonight when the stage darkened for Ardis's final confrontation with Kreton, and Cameron and I, and the middle-aged people who had played the Morelands were able to creep away.

We had to remain in costume until we had taken our bows, and it was nearly midnight

before Ardis and I got something to eat at the same small, dirty bar outside which Kreton had tried to rob me. Over the steaming plates she asked me if I had enjoyed acting, and I had to nod.

"I thought you would. Under all that solidity you're a very dramatic person, I think."

I admitted it was true, and tried to explain why I feel that what I call *the romance of life* is the only thing worth seeking. She did not understand me, and so I passed it off as the result of having been brought up on the *Shah Namah*, of which I found she had never heard.

We went to her apartment. I was determined to take her by force if necessary—not because I would have enjoyed brutalizing her, but because I felt she would inevitably think my love far less than it was if I permitted her to put me off a second time. She showed me about her quarters (two small rooms in great disorder), then, after we had lifted into place the heavy bar that is the sigil of every American dwelling, put her arms about me. Her breath was fragrant with the arrack I had bought for her a few minutes before. I feel sure now that for the rest of my life that scent will recall this evening to me.

When we parted, I began to unloose the laces that closed her blouse, and she at once pinched out the candle. I pleaded that she was thus depriving me of half the joy I might have had of her love; but she would not permit me to relight it, and our caresses and the embraces of our couplings were exchanged in perfect dark-

ness. I was in ecstasy. To have seen her, I would have blinded myself; yet nothing could have increased my delight.

When we separated for the last time, both spent utterly, and she left to wash, I sought for matches. First in the drawer of the unsteady little table beside the bed, then among the disorder of my own clothes, which I had dropped to the floor and we had kicked about. I found some eventually, but could not find the candle—Ardis, I think, had hidden it. I struck a match; but she had covered herself with a robe. I said, "Am I never to see you?"

"You will see me tomorrow. You're going to take me boating, and we'll picnic by the water, under the cherry trees. Tomorrow night the theater will be closed for Easter, and you can take me to a party. But now you are going home, and I am going to go to sleep." When I was dressed and standing in her doorway, I asked her if she loved me; but she stopped my mouth with a kiss.

I have already written about the rest— returning to find two eggs instead of three, and this book moved. I will not write of that again. But I have just—between this paragraph and the last—read over what I wrote earlier tonight, and it seems to me that one sentence should have had more weight than I gave it: when I said that in my role as Simon I never lost the *trend* of the play.

What the fabled secret buried by the old Americans beneath their carved mountain may be I do not know; but I believe that if it is some

key to the world of human life, it must be some form of that. Every great man, I am sure, consciously or not, in those terms or others, has grasped that secret—save that in the play that is our life we can grapple that trend and draw it to left or right if we have the will.

So I am doing now. If the taking of the egg was not significant, yet I will make it so—indeed I already have, when I infused one egg with the drug. If the scheme in which Ardis is entangled—with Golam Gassem and Mr. Tallman if it be they—is not some affair of statecraft and dark treasure, yet I will make it so before the end. If our love is not a great love, destined to live forever in the hearts of the young and the mouths of the poets, it will be so before the end.

Once again I am here; and in all truth I am beginning to wonder if I do not write this journal only to read it. No man was ever happier than I am now—so happy, indeed, that I was sorely tempted not to taste either of the two eggs that remain. What if the drug, in place of hallucination, self-knowledge, and euphoria, brings permanent and despairing madness? Yet I have eaten it nonetheless, swallowing the whole sweet lump in a few bites. I would rather risk whatever may come than think myself a coward. With equanimity I await the effects.

The fact is that I am too happy for all the Faustian determination I penned last night. (How odd that *Faust* will be the company's

next production. Kreton will be Mephistopheles of course—Ardis said as much, and it
would be certain in any case. Ardis herself will
be Margaret. But who will play the Doctor?)
Yet now, when all the teeth-gritting, table-
pounding determination is gone, I know that I
will carry out the essentials of the *plan* more
surely than ever—with the ease, in fact, of an
accomplished violinist sawing out some simple tune while his mind roves elsewhere. I have
been looking at the ruins of the Jeff (as they
call it), and it has turned my mind again to the
fate of the old Americans. How often they, who
chose their leaders for superficial appear-
ances of strength, wisdom, and resolution,
must have elected them only because they
were as fatigued as I was last night.

I had meant to buy a hamper of delicacies,
and call for Ardis about one, but she came for
me at eleven with a little basket already
packed. We walked north along the bank of
the channel until we reached the ruins of the
old tomb to which I have already referred, and
the nearly circular artificial lake the Americans call the Basin. It is rimmed with flower-
ing trees—old and gnarled, but very beautiful
in their robes of white blossom. For some little American coin we were given command of
a bright blue boat with a sail twice or three
times the size of my handkerchief, in which to
dare the halcyon waters of the lake.

When we were well away from the people on
shore, Ardis asked me, rather suddenly, if I

intended to spend all my time in America here in Washington.

I told her that my original plan had been to stay here no more than a week, then make my way up the coast to Philadelphia and the other ancient cities before I returned home; but that now that I had met her I would stay here forever if she wished it.

"Haven't you ever wanted to see the interior? This strip of beach we live on is kept half alive by the ocean and the trade that crosses it; but a hundred miles inland lies the wreck of our entire civilization, waiting to be plundered."

"Then why doesn't someone plunder it?" I asked.

"They do. A year never passes without someone bringing some great prize out—but it is so large . . ." I could see her looking beyond the lake and the fragrant trees. "So large that whole cities are lost in it. There was an arch of gold at the entrance to St. Louis—no one knows what became of it. Denver, the Mile High City, was nested in silver mines; no one can find them now."

"Many of the old maps must still be in existence."

Ardis nodded slowly, and I sensed that she wanted to say more than she had. For a few seconds there was no sound but the water lapping against the side of the boat.

"I remember having seen some in the museum in Teheran—not only our maps, but some of your own from a hundred years ago."

"The courses of the rivers have changed," she said. "And when they have not, no one can be sure of it."

"Many buildings must still be standing, as they are here, in the Silent City."

"That was built of stone—more solidly than anything else in the country. But yes, some, many, are still there."

"Then it would be possible to fly in, land somewhere, and pillage them."

"There are many dangers, and so much rubble to look through that anyone might search for a lifetime and only scratch the surface."

I saw that talking of all this only made her unhappy, and tried to change the subject. "Didn't you say that I could escort you to a party tonight? What will that be like?"

"Nadan, I have to trust someone. You've never met my father, but he lives close to the hotel where you are staying, and has a shop where he sells old books and maps." (So I had visited the right house—almost—after all!) "When he was younger, he wanted to go into the interior. He made three or four trips, but never got farther than the Appalachian foothills. Eventually he married my mother and didn't feel any longer than he could take the risks . . ."

"I understand."

"The things he had sought to guide him to the wealth of the past became his stock in trade. Even today, people who live farther inland bring him old papers; he buys them and resells them. Some of those people are only a

step better than the ones who dig up the cemeteries for the wedding rings of the dead women."

I recalled the rings I had bought in the shadow of the broken obelisk, and shuddered, though I do not believe Ardis observed it.

"I said that some of them were hardly better than the grave robbers. The truth is that some are worse—there are people in the interior who are no longer people. Our bodies are poisoned—you know that, don't you? All of us Americans. They have adapted—that's what Father says—but they are no longer human. He made his peace with them long ago, and he trades with them still."

"You don't have to tell me this."

"Yes I do—I must. Would you go into the interior, if I went with you? The government will try to stop us if they learn of it, and to confiscate anything we find."

I assured her with every oath I could remember that with her beside me I would cross the continent on foot if need be.

"I told you about my father. I said that he sells the maps and records they bring him. What I did not tell you is that he reads them first. He has never given up, you see, in his heart."

"He has made a discovery?" I asked.

"He's made many—hundreds. Bobby and I have used them. You remember those men in the restaurant? Bobby went to each of them with a map and some of the old letters. He's persuaded them to help finance an expedition

into the interior, and made each of them believe that we'll help him cheat the other—that keeps them from combining to cheat us, you see."

"And you want me to go with you?" I was beside myself with joy.

"We weren't going to go at all—Bobby was going to take the money, and go to Baghdad or Marrakesh, and take me with him. But, Nadan," here she leaned forward, I remember, and took my hands in hers, "there really is a secret. There are many, but one better—more likely to be true, more likely to yield truly immense wealth than all the others. I know you would share fairly with me. We'll divide everything, and I'll go back to Teheran with you."

I know that I have never been more happy in my life than I was then, in that silly boat. We sat together in the stern, nearly sinking it, under the combined shade of the tiny sail and Ardis's big straw hat, and kissed and stroked one another until we would have been pilloried a dozen times in Iran.

At last, when I could bear no more unconsummated love, we ate the sandwiches Ardis had brought, and drank some warmish, fruit-flavored beverage, and returned to shore.

When I took her home a few minutes ago, I very strongly urged her to let me come upstairs with her; I was on fire for her, sick to impale her upon my own flesh and pour myself into her as some mad god before the coming of the Prophet might have poured his golden blood into the sea. She would not per-

mit it—I think because she feared that her apartment could not be darkened enough to suit her modesty. I am determined that I will yet see her.

I have bathed and shaved to be ready for the party, and as there is still time I will insert here a description of the procession we passed on the way back from the lake. As you see, I have not yet completely abandoned the thought of a book of travels.

A very old man—I suppose a priest—carried a cross on a long pole, using it as a staff, and almost as a crutch. A much younger one, fat and sweating, walked backward before him swinging a smoking censer. Two robed boys carrying large candles preceded them, and they were followed by more robed children, singing, who fought with nudges and pinches when they felt the fat man was not watching them.

Like everyone else, I have seen this kind of thing done much better in Rome; but I was more affected by what I saw here. When the old priest was born, the greatness of America must have been a thing of such recent memory that few can have realized it had passed forever; and the entire procession—from the flickering candles in clear sunshine, to the dead leader lifted up, to his inattentive, bickering followers behind—seemed to me to incarnate the philosophy and the dilemma of these people. So I felt, at least, until I saw that they watched it as uncomprehendingly as they

might if they themselves were only travelers abroad, and I realized that its ritualized plea for life renewed was more foreign to them than to me.

It is very late—three, my watch says.

I resolved again not to write in this book. To burn it or tear it to pieces, or to give it to some beggar; but now I am writing once again because I cannot sleep. The room reeks of my vomit, though I have thrown open the shutters and let in the night.

How could I have loved that? (And yet a few moments ago, when I tried to sleep, visions of Ellen pursued me back to wakefulness.)

The party was a masque, and Ardis had obtained a costume for me—a fantastic gilded armor from the wardrobe of the theater. She wore the robes of an Egyptian princess, and a domino. At midnight we lifted our masks and kissed, and in my heart I swore that tonight the mask of darkness would be lifted too.

When we left, I carried with me the bottle we had brought, still nearly half full; and before she pinched out the candle I persuaded her to pour out a final drink for us to share when the first frenzy of our desire was past. She—it—did as I asked, and set it on the little table near the bed. A long time afterward, when we lay gasping side by side, I found my pistol with one groping hand and fired the beam into the wide-bellied glass. Instantly it filled with blue fire from the burning alcohol. Ardis screamed, and sprang up.

* * *

I ask myself now how I could have loved; but then, how could I in one week have come so near to loving this corpse-country? Its eagle is dead—Ardis is the proper symbol of its rule.

One hope, one very small hope remains. It is possible that what I saw tonight was only an illusion, induced by the egg. I know now that the thing I killed before Ardis's father's house was real, and between this paragraph and the last I have eaten the last egg. If hallucinations now begin, I will know that what I saw by the light of the blazing arrack was in truth a thing with which I have lain, and in one way or another will see to it that I never return to corrupt the clean wombs of the women of our enduring race. I might seek to claim the miniatures of our heritage after all, and allow the guards to kill me—but what if I were to succeed? I am not fit to touch them. Perhaps the best end for me would be to travel alone into this maggot-riddled continent; in that way I will die at fit hands.

Later. Kreton is walking in the hall outside my door, and the tread of his twisted black shoe jars the building like an earthquake. I heard the word *police* as though it were thunder. My dead Ardis, very small and bright, has stepped out of the candle-flame, and there is a hairy face coming through the window.

The old woman closed the notebook. The younger woman, who had been read-

ing over her shoulder, moved to the other side of the small table and seated herself on a cushion, her feet politely positioned so that the soles could not be seen. "He is alive then," she said.

The older woman remained silent, her gray head bowed over the notebook, which she held in both hands.

"He is certainly imprisoned, or ill; otherwise he would have been in touch with us." The younger woman paused, smoothing the fabric of her chador with her right hand, while the left toyed with the gem simulator she wore on a thin chain. "It is possible that he has already tried, but his letters have miscarried."

"You think this is his writing?" the older woman asked, opening the notebook at random. When the younger did not answer she added, "Perhaps. Perhaps."